D1371363

Sarah's Chance

Lauren Jan Craft

Copyright © 2020 Lauren Jan Craft

All rights reserved

The characters and events portrayed in this book are fictitious. Any similarity to
real persons, living or dead, is coincidental and not intended by the author.

No part of this book may be reproduced, or stored in a retrieval system, or
transmitted in any form or by any means, electronic, mechanical, photocopying,
recording, or otherwise, without express written permission of the publisher.

ISBN-13: 9798567127551
ISBN-10: 1477123456

Front Cover design by:
Melody Simmons-https://bookcoverscre8tive.com/
Library of Congress Control Number: 2018675309
Printed in the United States of America

To my wonderfully supportive husband, Roger, and my patient children, Eric, Ryan, Josh and Lauren who watched and waited as I scribbled for years...thank you!

Contents

Willows
By The
Watercourses

" For I will pour water upon him that is thirsty, and streams upon the dry ground.
I will pour My spirit upon thy seed, and blessings upon thy offspring:
And they shall spring up among the grass,
as willows by the watercourses."

-Isaiah 44:3-4

Prologue

In the trenches west of Atlanta, August the 3rd, 1864

Miss Sarah Partin,
　It is my sorrowful duty to inform you of the death of your brother William who was killed in a charge on the 22nd day of July last. This is a very painful thing to me and I know it will be heartrending to you this being the fifth brother you have lost since this cruel war commenced. It is hard but it seems to be the will of the all wise Creator and we must submit to it. Your brother was killed near the breastworks of the enemy. The command being compelled to fall back he was not buried by us but was buried by the enemy. As we found after we gained the ground all that he had was lost with him. Be assured in your grief that you have my own and the sympathies of the entire company. William was beloved by all the boys. There is something due him from the government which I will attend to just as soon as this campaign is over. I will close. I remain your closer friend.
B. F. Toomer

Sarah trembled holding the dreaded letter. Tears

stained the sky-blue paper with the terrible words. William. Dead. The last of five older brothers, the one whose deep baritone voice rang out in harmony as the congregation sang on meeting day, "Shall we gather at the river that flows by the throne of God." How could an all wise Creator take her parents, then her brothers one by one, and finally William, across that river and leave her here?

She sank to the rough boards of the porch clutching the damp letter, and silently cried out her heart to God. Rocking in mute rhythm to the waves of sorrow crashing upon her soul, she questioned—argued—then finally conceded that she must bear another blow with His help. She stilled as the normal sounds of nature quieted, as if in respect for her grief on display.

Eyes closed; she silently breathed a prayer for strength to go forward. Then, with new determination, she grasped the railing and pulled to her feet. She swiped the tears from her cheeks and scrubbed the moisture from her hands into the folds of her threadbare skirt.

Once again, she would have to tell Carrie and Gray grim news. She did not know if they would comprehend the implication regarding the farm and life as it had been. With no men of the family left to return to take up the management, the struggle to hold the land could be in vain.

She raised tear-swollen eyes to the cloudless sky that belied the dark and heavy burden she bore, "God give me the strength to bear what must be borne. Help me to know the words to say to Carrie and Gray. Help me to tend their grief." She choked back another sob, composed herself and entered the house.

Soft chatter, punctuated with seldom-heard laughter, accompanied her approach to the parlor. The swift change of expression on each of her siblings' faces as she entered the room told Sarah that her tears communicated all, before she had to speak the horrible words.

"No." Carrie breathed the word as if it would forestall reality. "No, no, no, no." She wailed her grief.

Sarah rushed to gather her sister into her arms and tried to soothe her as best she could with soft words. For four long years, she protected her siblings from some of the realities they faced. How could she protect them from this new grief? How could she survive it herself?

"How did it happen? When?" Gray's face was a stony mask.

"He was defending the outer breastworks surrounding Atlanta, July 22."

"He's been dead for over a month? It's a mistake! Let me see the letter." He reached for the crumpled blue page in Sarah's hand.

His eyes misted, reading the letter. "What will we do, Sarah?" Gray sank to the worn settee, his eyes searching hers for reassurance that she was not sure she could give.

"We will carry on as before. It is what Daddy and Mama and the boys would want." She had no idea how she might accomplish this stated plan. Carrie wept in her lap, beyond hearing the bold words.

Moans of grief filled the room for yet another of the dwindling Partin family. Despite the hard blow once again challenging her faith, Sarah sought the comforting presence of the Holy Spirit as she tended Carrie and Gray. She prayed for relief from such hard testing, though no end seemed in sight.

Chapter 1

Itawamba County, Mississippi 1866

Sarah pushed the sun-blocking straw hat back onto her shoulders and wiped the moisture threatening her eyes onto her sleeve. Leaning on the rickety fence and staring out across the dandelion pocked lawn to the fields beyond, dark thoughts surfaced. There was no help for it but to advertise for hired hands to plant, again.

She thought of the labor-intensive operation of getting the seeds into the ground. The job could not be embarked upon by two women and a half-grown boy. Most of the livestock was sold to refill the money box. The hogs were butchered to replenish the smoke-house, keeping only a few for breed stock. The milk cow, some chickens and the plow oxen were vital to sustain operations for the meantime. A good harvest would be essential for the farm to survive.

Wrapping her arms around her waist, she clutched the excess fabric draping across the front of a once perfectly fitted dress. A familiar shudder accompanied thoughts of defeat.

Gray trudged around the corner of the house and down the drive. Watching his approach, she read his mood in the march, fists clenched, head down. Life had been hard for him. Working alongside her and Carrie to keep a roof over their heads, and food on the table, he carried the weight of the Partin men lost to the war. He would never know the warmth of the large family that she once enjoyed.

His world consisted of watching war waged around him and having death take his brothers one man at a time. Until they were all gone. All the men who could guide him to his own manhood. She felt inadequate for that task.

"Any takers on our advertisement?" Gray cocked his dirt-stained face toward her.

"Not yet. The men are coming home but they have their own farms to tend. And besides, their holdings are all as worn down as ours." She reached out to brush a damp, blond lock from Gray's forehead. She felt more like a mother than a sister.

Gray looked toward the weather-beaten barn, as he paced back and forth. "Sarah, I don't see how we will get on if we don't get some help."

"God will provide. He will not desert us in our time of need." Sarah repeated her mother's often stated conviction although now she was not sure she had the same faith to believe it. All signs pointed to the opposite, that He had deserted them already.

"The same God that let Mama and Daddy and our brothers die and left us alone to fend for ourselves? Your faith is useless! It won't save this farm; it won't feed us!" He spat the words.

She understood his argument. He was weary

from doing the work of six men. She hoped that time would prove her right. She still clung to the belief that God made all things work together for good.

Wasn't that what William had written over four years from the battlefield before he finally followed his brothers in death?

He'd been her mentor in faith. He listened to her timid prayer asking Jesus to come into her heart when she was ten. She learned its tenets by watching her older brothers and her parents. They all lived their faith daily as they worked side by side in the fields, with the stock, and as they prayed each night at the evening meal for strength and endurance to meet the demands of another day.

Carrie and Gray were too young to remember that legacy of the Partin family, one of unfailing faith.

"I will not expect you to blindly accept my belief, but I only hope that you will come to see God is faithful. He does not shield us from evil and grief in the world, but He comforts us and gives us strength to endure all things with grace."

"I'm not feeling too comfortable," Gray snorted, holding out his blistered hands for her inspection.

Sarah took one bloodied hand and raised her apron to gently brush the grime from the wounds. "Help will come. God will provide."

Grunting his disgust for her lack of an active plan, other than to rely on her faith and the hope of help from strangers, he jerked his hand away and stomped back up the drive toward the barn.

Defeat again. She disliked losing a battle, let alone a war. Her own agitation rose. Could she carry on with grace when such problems threatened to engulf her family?

While the men served, they sent their small cash allotments home to help keep the farm and family fed. As each man died, small military pensions were sent. Now with the war over, the South was a conquered land.

The Confederate notes saved at William's insistence proved worthless, and the pensions ended. With no money coming in, except for what they could earn from livestock or crops, she stood to lose the farm. The rising taxes levied for reconstruction could not be paid. All the families in the small Fulton community were in the same fix.

She tried to hold her fears to herself in order to keep from alarming her siblings. Her carefree sister did not see a dark cloud unless it was poised above her. That cloud had come on those five awful days when Captain Toomer's letters arrived, each bringing the specter of death. When word came that Carrie's twin brother died, her cheery aspect changed. She now slipped through the days in quiet solemnity.

Gray seemed more aware of their peril, but Sarah tried to shield him from the harshest realities of the situation. The years of deprivation wore on her too. She spoke her frustration out loud, "God, can any good really come of all this?"

∞∞∞∞

The large trees lining the lane leading to the two-storied, frame house offered Jacob a respite from the mid-day sun. Grateful to God that he found the notice advertising for farm laborers at the livery, he made his way to the Partin farm. He chafed at the delay of another four months in his journey to Texas. Similar stops along the way from Alabama, some more profitable than others, left him still in need of a bigger cash stake in order to take care of his mother and his brother.

Perspiration slithered down his neck into his collar where it pooled to stain his only clean shirt. It was an unusually hot day for early spring. There would be a few more cool snaps, then the rains, before the real scorching settled in that would wring the energy from land, man and beast.

The house ahead must have been one of the better dwellings in the county before the war. Now the peeling paint and badly patched roof showed the lack of attention, or manpower, suffered during the war. Stretches of fencing lay on the ground. The lawn and fields grew a riot of mixed vegetation, mostly weeds. He surmised the men of this family had not come home, thus the advertisement for help with the planting.

Though he hated the idea of intruding on the heated exchange taking place between the boy and girl in the drive ahead, he had walked five miles from town, and he was not about to backtrack. As the girl became aware of his approach, she straightened, running her small, work-reddened hands over her disheveled hair and field clothes.

"Sir, may I help you?"

He raked his sweat-stained hat from his head seeing that this was no girl but a petite woman. She was so small it would be easy to mistake her for a child except for the intense stare she leveled at him.

"I've come about the advertisement posted at the livery. Are you Miss Sarah Partin?" He heard her sigh as she scanned him from head to toe and her expression relaxed somewhat.

"I am. I believe I made my needs known in the posting so if you feel you are up to it then the job is yours. There is a spare room upstairs. I'll warn you that our food is meager, and only me, my sister and brother to help."

Worse than he thought but what choice did he have? The small compensation offered, to be taken in milk, eggs and garden vegetables, would help feed them until the harvest in late June when he would be paid a small dividend from the sale of the crop.

"I accept the conditions and the offer of the room. I have but one request. I know this will sound forward but you see, Ma'am, I am at my last resort. My mother and wounded brother are along, and I must feed and shelter them as well. Now I will be glad to do so out of my own share at no extra expense to you if they can just come and be on the place with me. My brother and I have a tent we can use, but I would be obliged if you would allow my mother to take the room." Jacob spoke quickly, twisting his hat in his hands.

Miss Partin seemed contemplative, no sign of shock at such a request. He detected no prejudice. The times dictated that people who would never dream of being reduced to begging, now wandered the countryside in search of kindness from strangers.

As her gaze swept over him again, he resisted the urge to straighten his frayed, sweat soaked collar and scrub the toes of his dusty boots on the back of his faded pants. The need to beg shamed him, but he would do what was necessary for his family.

Suddenly she braced. She drew herself up as tall as she could muster. No doubt this stance was developed especially for the Yankee and Confederate raiders who came to conscript her horses and food staples.

"If you are driven to ask such favors of a total stranger then circumstances must be hard indeed. I understand hard circumstances well. I will accept this unusual arrangement but won't allow any shirking at my family's expense. I expect hard labor for small pay and no distractions from your work."

"Ma'am, I am at your service and in your debt. I will return tomorrow if that is convenient." Jacob took a step back.

His new employer nodded her agreement. "It is. Tomorrow then."

Turning to head back down the drive, he could sense her gaze at his back. He breathed a silent prayer of thanks to God for the generosity of this woman. He vowed to make her life a bit easier for it.

∞ ∞ ∞

The tall stranger with the compelling eyes trudged back up the road. She'd forgotten to get his name. The sad state of his clothes and the gaunt look common to all the returning Confederate soldiers tugged at her heart. She imagined her brothers in such a situation if they had survived.

She relaxed her tightly drawn stance. Weariness swept over her. The heavy weight of responsibility for her kin, increased by this man and his family, bore down. If the stranger walking away meant any harm, then she would surrender to it for she had no will left to deny him the work he seemed to desperately need.

Chapter 2

"Jacob, I will not hear of it! I cannot impose myself on complete strangers." Cordelia McKenna brushed wisps of snow-white hair from her flushed face. She tended a kettle of watery vegetable stew dangling over a campfire of scrawny twigs.

"Mama, I will see a roof over your head before the spring rains come. And what of Charles? His wound still looks angry. He must have better food, or he'll never heal." Jacob kept his voice low to keep from informing all the fellow citizens in the hastily erected tent-city of his frustration with his strong-willed mother.

Cordelia straightened, her hands kneading her back. "I know son, I just cannot get used to such a turn of fortune. I know we must depend on others for our keep now. I must depend on you. I'm sorry. I can stay in the wagon as I have done these past months."

Jacob noted the tears threatening to spill from her darkly circled eyes as she turned away to stir the pitiful offering she prepared for supper. She had always been strong, the quiet force behind their father, leader of the McKenna clan, and their spiritual guide. When times were hard, she worked hard and prayed harder, creating an indelible example of reliance on God.

The war had worn her down. Jacob grieved to see the slump in her proud shoulders. She moved at a slow-motion pace to complete tasks that in the past she did in a snap, accompanied by her lilting hum of old Highland melodies. He desperately hoped that the move out of the crowded refugee camp would help his mother and brother to recover.

He moved closer and rested a hand on her shoulder, a clumsy attempt at comfort. "I am the head of our family now and I have a responsibility to make sure you are provided for. We need to go. Please take the room offered. I could not bear to lose more of my family for lack of shelter."

Cordelia reached around his waist and gave him a soft hug. "I will do what you wish."

∞∞∞

Jacob turned and stepped inside the tent to check on Charles. He settled on a small canvas stool, observing his brother as he napped. It reminded him of the years he shared the sunny, second-story room at home in Alabama. Carefree and happy then, with loving parents, a fine home, and plenty of food to eat, he worked hard from an early age with his family. There was a common goal of improving the land for future generations that would inherit the fruit of the combined labor.

Marching out of town at the beginning of the war with his childhood friends to the fanfare of cheers, and the tears of his young sweetheart, he vowed to return within a month. Now Father and the land were gone, and he was left to start over. Friends were buried in hasty graves all up and down the battlegrounds of the South. His sweetheart married a man who stayed behind. The conflict brought with it a realization that war is unspeakably cruel, some men are without honor and that a lifetime of hard work can be lost in a short four-year span.

He grieved for his mother who mourned the loss of her beloved husband shot by Yankee raiders. She faced authorities alone when they came to take the land while her sons lay wounded hundreds of miles from home. Jacob leaned over, propping his elbows on his knees. He bowed his head into his hands. All the wishing in the world would not retrieve the life he knew.

His mother's example taught him to take what comes and work with it. As soon as he realized that there was no land to return to, he cast about to find work to support his family. Most of the connections to whom he could apply for work were gone, displaced by the war. There were too many hungry and homeless and too few jobs to support them.

He set out, with his mother and wounded brother in tow, on the road filled with a multitude of displaced Confederates, plotting a course for Texas. Now stalled in Fulton due to lack of funds, Jacob searched for any odd job to refill the purse, as he did all along the way. Then he found the small, neatly hand-written advertisement posted at the general store.

The five-mile trek to the farm that morning changed his family's prospects considerably. He practically begged the slight woman in the baggy dress for work today. It was a position he never thought to find himself in, that of a homeless beggar. He now had a place to go, out of the camps, where there would be a room for Mama and food. And the promise of a stake to continue the trip to Texas where land advertised to be plentiful and cheap. A place to start over. Jacob let out a weary sigh. In the morning they would move to the Partin farm and another leg of the long journey to a new home and a new life would begin.

Charles moaned softly as he shifted in his sleep. A grimace accompanied his movements as he roused from his nap. He interrupted Jacob's dark thoughts, "Hey brother, why the long face?"

"Well look who decided to stir himself."

"Any luck?" Charles eased himself to a sitting position on the side of the cot.

Jacob observed his brother's slow, guarded movements and again the weight of regret sat heavily on his shoulders. He was unable to prevent the carnage the day the Yanks swarmed the hillside camp near Chattanooga, killing his best friend and leaving Charles among the wounded. His rational mind knew that he could not have made a difference in the outcome of that skirmish, but he felt guilty for not being able to protect his younger brother. He promised his mother he would watch over him.

"I got the job."

"What do you mean, *you* got the job? I thought you were offerin' us both for hire," Charles growled.

"Well I was, but I decided not to get their hopes up. We don't know how much longer you'll be needing to rest to get that leg healed."

"I guess you're right. But as soon as I can get around, I'm pitchin' in, you hear?" Charles massaged the swollen flesh on the edge of the reddened gash just above his right knee that would likely leave him with a limp for life.

"I did ask if Mama could take the room in the house that was offered. She was pretty riled that I was so forward, but she needs to be in a real bed at night."

"Good thinking, brother. She needs some relief from that wagon."

"We will stay in the tent, but I saw a broken down shed on the property. If we can repair it, I will ask if we can bed down there. We need to get a roof over your head too," Jacob teased, There was truth in his assessment that the tent was not shelter enough for him or his brother if they were to gain back the strength they had lost.

"I have been in this tent for six years, a few more give or take won't matter. We'll soon be in Texas where I'll build the biggest palace on the prairie. There will be rooms for us all and a new cook-stove for Mama," Charles expanded on the often talked about dream.

"Field crops as far as the eye can see."

"Cattle on a thousand hills," Charles quoted the old family Bible.

"And the Yankees thought they could keep a good man down." Jacob gave his brother a friendly jab in the shoulder. "We go out tomorrow."

Cordelia entered the tent with wooden bowls and the kettle of thin, steaming soup. Jacob's stomach rumbled. He had not eaten since breakfast. The family settled down to give thanks to God over the meager provision for one more day and for the promise of shelter, food and a stake for their intended journey if, tomorrow, God granted the strength to take the offer at the Partin farm.

∞∞∞

Sarah prayed over the evening meal of boiled eggs, red beans, rice and cornbread. It was a veritable feast compared to what most in the war-ravaged county had to sustain broken lives with.

"Heavenly Father, we thank you for the provision of food for the nourishment of our bodies. Make us mindful of the needs of others even as we bear our grief. Give us strength to carry on and to meet needs where we may." The vision of the tall stranger came to Sarah as she prayed. He seemed especially in need of help that morning and she sensed that to accept his offer to work was the right thing to do. "Father; lend your strength to the weary stranger that came today. Let his coming be a blessing to this household. Amen."

"So, you hired the man that came today?" Gray disengaged his hand and reached for the cornbread. "He didn't look like he could be much help."

"Well, he needs proper food to get his strength back," Sarah explained. "He has a brother who was wounded in the war and is still mending. He also has his mother to care for, so I agreed to allow them to come as well."

"Just invite the whole county to come and live off us, Sarah." Gray slapped his half-eaten bread to his plate.

"They won't be living off us. They will be working and earning their keep," Sarah corrected.

"They will still be taking food out of our mouths," Gray grumbled.

"Gray, we must do our share to help those who've lost everything. We still have our land and our home. These people obviously have nothing, but they are willing to work."

Gray gave up his protest with a shrug and devoured his supper.

Sarah's exasperation faded as her gaze shifted to her sister. Carrie ate slowly and quietly, her eyes on her plate, discouraging conversation. William's death was the final blow. He wrote faithfully during the four years of the war. He regaled them with stories of camp life and general conditions he encountered through the army's movements. He informed them of the death of Marion and John. Sarah wondered if there could ever be such joy in their lives again now that they were all gone. John, Marion, Ben, Sam and William...Mama and Daddy...it was so quiet at table these last six years. Now the silence would be forever.

Sarah lost her appetite. She rose from the large oak table that seemed so deserted with only three of them dining and left the room. The squeak of the wooden plank floor marked her passage across the wide hall to the cloak tree where she recovered her light cotton shawl. She left the silent house to stand at the porch railing to watch the sunset. Pink and purple hues splayed across the barren fields. The beauty of the evening enveloped Sarah and her jangled nerves began to calm.

A dove called to its life-mate, breaking the silence. The pair at the edge of the yard stayed close to one another as they searched for their evening meal. She thought of her intended mate, James. He left with William to join her brothers at the beginning of the war and like her brothers, James had not returned. He died early on so she was over the shock, but the ache of loneliness for her love lost could sometimes be evoked by a memory or a reminder such as the doves' devotion to one another.

With most of the men gone from the county now and the rest leaving for new land farther west, her chances of finding a new life-mate were slim. A lone tear spilled over Sarah's thick, dark lashes and trailed down her cheek before she dabbed it ruthlessly with the end of her shawl. She had not cried since the day Captain Toomer's last letter came and she was not going to weep for things she could not have. She would live in the here and now with the lot she was dealt. For better or worse, the refugee and his family would arrive tomorrow and, her family would begin to rebuild their home and land...with God's help.

Chapter 3

Jacob splashed cold water from the bucket onto his face and neck. The brisk morning air helped shake the effects of the restless night. He coaxed a bit of lather from a tiny sliver of soap across his broad chest to freshen up before leaving for the Partin farm. As he washed, he felt the change in his body due to the privation of years of camp life. He lost twenty pounds and a lot of brawn. Months in a field hospital also took their toll. He hoped the labor on the farm would help him to regain his former strength. When finished with his morning rinsing, he made his way to the tent to wake the others. After loading the wagons with their few possessions, they said their good-byes to those who shared the misery of refugee life with them.

"Don't forget to check back with us in August, Jake," a craggy-faced old-timer admonished. "We'll be formin' the train for Texas then and want to see ya'll on it."

Jacob nodded and waved as he guided the horses onto the hard-packed dirt road leading west of town. At noon the wagon wound its way up the tree-lined lane leading to the house. A columned porch wrapped around the east side facing a large stable and various out-buildings. Jacob could see by the look in his Mama's eyes that the large house reminded her of a more prosperous time when they owned a similar home and thought their comfortable existence would never end.

As he drew the wagon to a halt before the front steps, Miss Partin appeared at the doorway. Unlike the day before when he had surprised her in her field clothes with her honey-colored hair flying about her head, today she wore a pale blue dress that emphasized her eyes and her unruly tresses were neatly pulled back from her small oval face. Just a few tendrils escaped at her temples. She was child-like in stature but clearly a woman in form. The sight of Miss Partin in her neat Sunday best was pleasant indeed.

He was embarrassed to arrive in such an unkempt condition. He felt worse when he observed his mother's efforts to straighten her wrinkled skirt and threadbare blouse. He glanced back at Charles who managed a weak smile, indicating he could hold up a while longer before needing to rest from the bumpy ride.

Sarah held herself erect and smiled at the ragged group. They looked more needy than she was prepared to handle with her limited resources. The tall stranger looked cleaner, probably because today he had the advantage of riding as opposed to walking.

Observing the older woman's downcast eyes as

she smoothed her hands over her disheveled clothing, she somehow knew this woman had been used to better. She wanted to calm her unease but did not know how to do so without giving offense.

Only one of these people looked capable of helping with the chores and field work. She was going from the frying pan into the fire in terms of responsibility to feed and shelter those in her care. Nevertheless, they had arrived. She would deal with the situation as best she could.

"You have returned as promised." Sarah tried to sound calm. She moved to the top of the steps but did not descend. She knew her small stature would diminish the command she tried to affect in her voice.

The hired man jumped from the wagon seat and went to the opposite side to help his mother down. He took her arm and escorted her carefully up the steps. "Miss Partin, I would like to introduce my mother, Cordelia McKenna."

"I am very pleased to meet you, Mrs. McKenna."

"And I am pleased to meet you as well." Cordelia smiled, soft lines crinkling around her eyes.

Sarah offered her hand and as she took Cordelia's, offered in return, a peace settled over her. She felt in her spirit that this woman would be someone special to her. It was a strange kind of knowing that only God can impart. Sarah accepted it as a sign that, despite misgivings, she did the right thing in bringing this family into her home.

Turning to the man whose presence beside her, in contrast, was disturbing, she extended her hand to him as well. "Sir, I do not believe I got your name."

Jacob took her work-roughened hand in his. She was embarrassed by the calluses on what should have been smooth skin. He looked directly into her eyes, as if to pledge by his honor that he would help her and her family to recoup what he could not for his own. "Jacob McKenna, at your service."

Pulling her hand away, she averted her eyes from that unsettling stare. She could feel a flush rising from the embroidered collar of her dress to the top of her head. It was not her way to be so easily flustered. She hurriedly escorted Cordelia to the door. Turning, she saw that Jacob was helping his brother to the shade of a nearby tree. Raising her voice to carry across the yard she called, "Please sir, come into the house for some refreshments before you settle in."

Seeming surprised by the offer, Jacob hesitated then returned. With no apparent effort he carried his brother up the steps. "This is Charles. I will be obliged if you will point out where you wish for us to set up our accommodations and I will get to it and be ready to start with any work you need done today."

"Ah, the younger brother. Pleased to meet you. We can discuss arrangements while we have some lunch." She opened the screen door and held it while Jacob brought his sibling into the house as Cordelia carefully guided the injured limb through the passageway.

Sarah ushered them into the front parlor that was her mother's pride and joy. Leading Cordelia and Charles to the worn brocade sofa, she provided a small petite-point covered stool to prop the injured leg.

When the family was settled, she made her way to the kitchen where Carrie prepared a light lunch of smoked ham sandwiches and preserved peaches. The slivers of meat and fruit were the last in their store from the fall.

Carrie looked lovely in the pale green muslin dress that set off her golden hair and creamy skin. She begged her sister to take extra pains with her appearance for the new family's arrival. Carrie had neglected it in recent weeks. She wanted her family to always put their best foot forward regardless of circumstances.

"If we had more sugar and some lemons, we could have made lemonade," Carrie mused to herself as she pumped cool water into the serving pitcher.

"I just pray for this fickle weather to cooperate so that the garden might make earlier. Otherwise, I do not know what we will eat besides the beans in the cellar. At least we have plenty of them," Sarah stated the reality of the situation.

Returning to the parlor with the trays, she watched as Carrie's gaze flickered over the tall man standing behind the sofa before lighting on the wounded one seated. Carrie always championed runts-of-the-litter and all things wounded. Her blank expression changed to one of concern as she observed him.

Sarah moved silently among the cushioned chairs to help Carrie serve the refreshments before seating herself near the small secretary by the window to catch the intermittent breeze.

"Miss Partin?" Cordelia broke the awkward silence.

"Oh, please, call me Sarah."

"Yes...Sarah, I had a similar pattern of wallpaper in my front parlor at home," Cordelia reflected with a wistful smile.

Sarah wasn't surprised at this revelation as it confirmed to her that Cordelia had not always lived a vagabond life but was reduced to it.

"My mother loved floral patterns. You will notice them throughout the house. I am afraid some of the furnishings and papers are in sad need of repair as my brother and sister and I have been alone these past five years. Keeping the farm chores done has absorbed our time. With the war over, I hope we can set things back right with the farm so that we can refurbish the house properly."

"My dear, it is fine, just fine. You have done an admirable job. I do not want to pry but I assume your parents have departed this life?" Cordelia asked.

"Yes, they were both taken with cholera before the war. And then our older brothers served the Confederacy."

"You had brothers serving with the Confederacy, Miss Partin?" Jacob sat forward to inquire.

"Yes, Mr. McKenna...five." Sarah shifted under his gaze.

"And when do you expect them back?" Jacob continued what seemed an interrogation. Perhaps he was worried he had just gotten employment only to lose it when the men of the house returned. She spoke quietly but the depth of emotion that spilled forth in her raw statement surprised her. "They will not be back, sir. They have all lost their lives in this senseless conflict."

Choking back a sob, Carrie shot up from the rocker in the corner where she had retired from the group and fled the room.

Sarah rose to follow.

"I am deeply sorry, Miss Partin, I did not intend to reopen such a fresh wound," Jacob apologized.

Sarah faced him and, observing the stricken look on his face, softened the retort she felt on the tip of her tongue. "It is alright, Mr. McKenna. Even grievous wounds heal with time." Her gaze swept the shocked faces of his mother and brother. Then she hurried after her sister and crashed headlong into Gray as he came bounding into the room at that inopportune moment.

"Where have you been? I asked you to be here by noon." Sarah whispered as her gaze raked him from head to toe. "You are filthy as well. Go at once and wash up. I'll expect you back here in a quarter hour."

She turned Gray around and pushed him out of the room ahead of her. "Excuse us for the moment if you don't mind," she called over her shoulder.

∞∞∞

What an inauspicious beginning. The McKenna's

must surely think her family lacking in good breeding and manners. She was especially careful to see that the rest of the afternoon and evening went well.

Gray cleaned up and presented himself on time. He managed to play a charming host as they toured the stables and outbuildings and laid out a site for the men's tent. She gave Jacob and Charles permission to repair the shed for their use as a more substantial shelter.

Gray passed the potatoes at supper when prompted. Polite conversation was still beyond his grasp, due to lack of practice. Carrie calmed herself and reasonably entertained at the table, responding to the attention of Charles.

Jacob ate silently, continuing to observe her as she served the table then cleared it. By the time the meal was done, despite the success of the afternoon, Sarah was exhausted from acting under such intense scrutiny and from worrying what Carrie or Gray might do next. Local hired help being extremely difficult to find, it was essential to keep the McKenna's happy. Even if she was getting one for the price of three.

"Mrs. McKenna, I know you must be very tired." Sarah could see the circles beneath Cordelia's eyes. She had probably not had a good night's sleep in a while, displaced as she was.

"Yes, I believe I am ready to retire after that fine meal," Cordelia offered a compliment that surprised and gratified Sarah.

"I'll get Mother's things from the wagon." Jacob

scooted his chair out and unfolded his tall frame from the table. His gaze brushed the two women as he left the room.

"Gray, would you please go help Mr. McKenna," Sarah requested.

Gray bristled at the suggestion but did as he was told.

Sarah and Cordelia left Carrie and Charles, who were deep in conversation, to ascend the wide staircase leading to the second floor. Sarah took Cordelia's warm hand and again felt a kinship with this woman she could not define. It was as if she was escorting Mama, as she had done so many evenings before. Before the war...before death.

When they arrived at the landing, on an unexpected impulse, Sarah turned toward the spacious master bedroom that was her Mama's and Daddy's. She prepared a spare room for the hired man's mother but that was before she met Cordelia. She opened the door to her parents' room and led Cordelia inside.

Sarah knew that Cordelia immediately sensed she was in the main bedroom. She stopped abruptly inside the door and would not venture further.

"Oh, Sarah, I cannot accept this room. It is much too nice," Cordelia sighed as she surveyed the lovely bedchamber.

Unlike the rest of the house which showed signs of having been lived in, this room was well kept but clearly unused for some time. The late evening light filtered through the delicate lace curtains and dappled the large four-poster bed. The furnishings were light and simple in design.

"Mrs. McKenna, you must, I insist. It was my Mama's and Daddy's room. It is the best in the house. I think they would want you to enjoy it as they did." Sarah saw a tear trace down Cordelia's cheek.

Cordelia squeezed Sarah's hand. "I guessed as much and that is why I cannot take it. I could not impose in such a way."

Sarah turned to face Cordelia and grasped her other hand. "No, I really want you to have it. Please, you must take it."

As their gazes locked in friendly battle, Jacob interrupted the tense scene, trudging up the stairs carrying a large trunk on his shoulders.

"Over here, Mr. McKenna, to the left," Sarah called with a note of amusement in her voice. She won the first skirmish with the quietly proud Cordelia McKenna.

The son's face mirrored his mother's earlier reaction as he entered what was undoubtedly the main bedroom. "Are you sure, Miss Partin?" Jacob queried with a skeptical look on his face.

"Yes, quite certain." Sarah broke contact with Cordelia and rushed to the foot of the bed. "Please put the trunk here," she directed, her eyes once again locking with Cordelia's, asserting her victory.

Jacob lowered the trunk then straightened to survey the comfortable room. "This is very nice, Miss Partin. I thank you on behalf of my mother. This appears to be the master's room. Are you sure this is the room we discussed?" Jacob's direct question demanded an honest answer.

"No, Mr. McKenna, it is not." Sarah lifted her chin, confronting his intimidating stare. "That was before I met your mother."

Jacob stood motionless, assessing his small benefactress with new respect. She was gracious to them upon their arrival. She treated them as guests, not as hired help. She set her table with her best things and fed them the best meal they had eaten in weeks. She did all this with the command of a general over her small troops; her brother and sister seemed to submit to her authority. Yet she had compassion, as her gesture toward his mother suggested. Impressed with her ability to persuade by mere force of will, without argument, Jacob capitulated.

After settling Cordelia into her new quarters, Sarah quietly descended the stairs to find Charles and Carrie still engaged in animated conversation over the checkerboard that was always set ready for a game. She thought this strange since Carrie had been so quiet over the past few months. Yet any change for the better was welcome. She was glad to hear voices, it had been silent for too long.

She wandered out onto the porch in time to see a streak of lightning slash the darkening sky in the distance. She fervently prayed that the storm would track to the east and not pelt the newcomers tonight.

A short distance from the house she could see Jacob erecting the worn camp tent that would be his, and his brother's, shelter until they could repair the shed. Sarah felt a nagging discomfort at the thought of leaving them to the outside elements. It was Mr. McKenna's idea, so she allowed it to stand.

There was no wasted motion in his work. As ravaged as his body appeared, he was still strong enough to carry his brother. Quick and deliberate, he had the tent site ready in less than a half hour. He strode to the house when finished. Sarah was embarrassed to be caught with her gaze fixed on him as he ascended the steps.

He looked directly back into her eyes. "I'll get my brother now, looks like a storm moving in." He held the door for her. She felt his presence at her back as she led him to collect Charles.

"Charles, time to turn in." Jacob moved to his brother's chair to pick him up.

Charles winked playfully at Carrie, issuing a challenge. "We will resume tomorrow?"

"Indeed," Carrie returned a dimpled smile.

"Good evening, Miss Partin," Jacob offered as he eased past Sarah, his arm brushing hers as she held the outside door. A static spark snapped all her senses to attention as she watched him go.

Late that night, after the quick but intense spring storm moved on, Sarah heard the music for the first time. It drifted over the humid night air into her room as she tossed restlessly under the light cotton comforter. The haunting tune wound around her like magician's smoke, curling and twisting. Expertly played on a finely tuned fiddle, the sweet notes stirred memories of her lost love James' and her brother's playing and of a life she could never retrieve. When the ache in her heart seemed unbearable, the music ended, and the gentle night sounds lulled her into exhausted sleep.

Chapter 4

Sarah awoke to the sound of pans rattling and cupboards being pillaged. The smell of hot coffee and frying bacon assaulted her senses. She hurried to wash, pull on her work clothes and descended the stairs to the kitchen to find Cordelia mumbling about "biscuit fixins" as she searched the pantry. "Mrs. McKenna, please don't bother, I will get breakfast."

"Now, my dear, just save your breath. I am not one to lay about and eat up your victuals without doin' a lick of work. I will pull my weight as you have been so gracious to open your home to us."

Sarah could see by the determined look in Cordelia's eyes that this was a battle she could not win. She smiled in resignation. "Very well, Mrs. McKenna. But you must allow me to help you at least."

"Only if you drop that Mrs. nonsense and call me Cordelia."

"Yes, Ma'am."

Cordelia quirked her brow.

"Cordelia," Sarah corrected.

Sarah set the table as Cordelia efficiently prepared a breakfast feast from the meager supplies on hand. Her mouth watered at the sight of the food laid out on the sideboard: bacon, light oatcakes, fluffy biscuits, her own celebrated peach preserves, scrambled eggs, buttery hominy grits, with coffee to wash the hearty meal down. The give and take with Cordelia preparing the meal reminded Sarah of the wonderful times she had shared with her mother in this kitchen. An ache of sadness squeezed her heart until the McKenna men appeared as if by magic. Jacob carried a wide-awake Charles and deposited him in a chair. He then slipped outside and returned with two pails of fresh warm milk. Carrie and Gray appeared, drawn by the delicious aromas.

When they were all seated, Sarah ventured to offer a belated thanks for the milk. "Mr. McKenna."

"Please call me Jacob," his deep voice resonated through the room.

"Uh...Jacob," Sarah hesitated. "Thank you for doing the milking. It is my least favorite chore." She was still slightly unnerved by the intensity with which he studied her across the plates heaped with biscuits and eggs.

A small grin played at the corners of his mouth. "You are welcome, Miss Partin. I will relieve you of that chore permanently as of now. I do intend to earn my keep."

Before Sarah could reply, Cordelia asked, "Jacob, would you bless the food." She looked to Sarah for approval.

Sarah's gaze swept around the crowded table before she nodded her consent and closed her eyes for the blessing. Jacob's masculine voice filled the room as he blessed the food and prayed God's protection over the household.

She breathed a prayer of thanks as well, for it seemed these people who had invaded her world would indeed bless her family with their coming. It was apparent that, rather than three people for the price of one, the McKennas would be well worth her investment.

Sarah looked up to find the bright light of Jacob's eyes blazing upon her. Again, she felt the strange sensation of knowing. This time it was that this man would affect her life, but in what way she could not fathom.

∞ ∞ ∞

Over the next weeks, work began to repair the fences and badly worn structures. Spring planting started with hope for a good harvest to restore finances. Sarah stood from her stooped position over the rows of furrowed earth to mop the perspiration that threatened to spill over her brows into her already stinging eyes. She looked out at the other figures toiling in the freshly plowed field to drop and cover the seed. At intervals among the rows were Gray, Carrie, Cordelia and Charles slowly making their way up the pathways created by Jacob maneuvering the plow. This acreage would be corn field with any luck. Other fields would be sown for wheat and hay.

Sarah watched Jacob work. His recovering muscles bunched beneath the damp linen shirt as he gee-hawed the oxen to guide the plow in a straight row. He seemed to never tire. Hour after hour he kept at it; plowing, mending the farm tools, tack or fences, repairing the outbuildings and the house.

He was up before dawn to tend the stock and retired only after completing all possible chores he could set his hand to that day. Jacob McKenna marked a blinding pace. She could do no less than to meet it. She fell into step working, if not at the same vicious pace, at least close to it.

Later in the day, Sarah shielded her eyes, squinting upward, to see that the sun was more than over-head. She called out to Gray, closest to her, to signal the others to break for the mid-day meal. Stiffly she stepped over the freshly planted corn toward the wagon.

Retrieving the basket of food, she headed for a small patch of blessed shade under the pecan trees near the edge of the field and spread an old, soft quilt on the lone patch of grass. Before passing the food, she nodded to Jacob to say grace. It seemed odd to turn to a practical stranger for this family duty, but it was becoming routine practice.

"Heats gettin' up there," Charles remarked, finally breaking the silence between bites of his mother's golden cornbread and swigs of cool water.

"Are you holdin' up alright?" Jacob scrutinized Charles for signs of fatigue.

"I'm fine Jake, the leg's still a little stiff, but I

can drop corn seed as good as the women!" Charles snapped.

Sarah sensed that Charles was still riled that he could not work the fields as he had before his injury. When they first arrived at the farm, he did anything that could be done sitting down, mending tack or repairing small items. As he gained strength, he struggled to exercise his weakened leg. His limp was pronounced, the wound was still susceptible to aggravation if over-stressed.

She tried to ease the tension by turning the conversation to the plain but delicious food. "Cordelia, thank you for preparing the basket. You really do too much."

"Nonsense, I do my share, that's all."

If the past few weeks were any example, Cordelia would quit the field at mid-afternoon to return to the kitchen to fix supper for the bone-tired laborers. Her insistence in taking on the preparation of the meals and the housework gave Sarah time to concentrate on the general management of the farm. Still, there was little time for rest.

"Are we goin' to the singin' Saturday?" Gray asked, his mouth stuffed with food.

"Don't talk with your mouth full," Sarah handed him a cloth to wipe the crumbs he had dribbled down his shirt. "I don't know how we can. We must finish the planting this week and we are only half done. Besides, you need to repair the harness before we can take the wagon to town again. I believe that was your job and you have stalled getting it done."

Gray huffed up and left the group. Sarah knew he was not enthused about the singing but wanted to meet his friends at the event for a bit of fun.

"You are too hard on him, Sarah. He's still a boy. He needs to have some fun again. Maybe the singin' would be good for us all," Carrie ventured hopefully as she began to pack up the remains of the meal.

All attention now focused on her reply. "He may be just a boy but, if we are to survive, he's got to begin accepting more responsibility for the needs of the family and farm. I don't wish it to be this way, it just is. And we have only a few more days to get the planting done."

Sarah's gaze followed Gray as he tramped down the rows toward the plow. It was his turn to give Jacob a brief reprieve. Then she scanned the hopeful looks fixed on her. "If we succeed, perhaps we can go."

The conversation buzzed with anticipation of a day of fun. "Well then, let's get back to it," Charles braced his hand against the tree trunk for support and awkwardly worked his way up then offered a hand to Carrie. Sarah watched as they wandered back to the field with their stomachs full and new energy for the arduous afternoon ahead. Jacob stood as well. He considered her for a moment before he nodded for a respectful withdrawal, then turned toward the creek to retrieve water for the animals.

∞∞∞

"You are a determined young woman, Sarah Partin," Cordelia challenged, leaning back on her knees.

"Pardon?" Sarah looked up in surprise.

"You work sunup to sundown, and you keep everyone else at it too. You tend to all the accounts and to all the details of running this farm, but do you ever do anything at all for yourself?" Cordelia's expression softened as she reached to touch Sarah's hand.

"I—I don't know what you mean," Sarah fumbled.

"Just that, perhaps, you could use an outing too. A girl your age needs a bit of socializing now and then."

Sarah looked Cordelia squarely in the eye. "I am not a girl. I am a full-grown woman and I have a charge to keep...to save this farm."

Her eyes gleamed with the surety of knowing, that it all depended on her.

Then she relaxed in the warmth of the growing smile on Cordelia's face. "I am sorry Cordelia," the words sighed from her lips as she slumped, her hands dropping from the restless gathering and putting away into her lap. "I know I am too intense at times. I just can't seem to relax. I have so much to tend to."

"I know dear, but we are here now. Let us take up some of your burden."

Sarah cocked her head, meeting Cordelia's soft gaze, "Thank you, I will try."

"And the singin'?" Cordelia grinned.

"I suppose we all could use some merriment." Sarah smiled as she knew she was being led into a trap but allowed herself to follow.

∞∞∞

Jacob took the plow from Gray and prepared to work the last rows for the day. He looked across the field to find Sarah. It was a habit he found developing despite his will to discourage it. She filled his thoughts more than was appropriate. He watched her as she commanded her small band which now included his family. They followed her lead in the attempt to retrieve what the hard years had taken. She never shirked from the hardest task.

He was used to the refined belles of the south and she clearly had lived that life once. Now she stooped to drop seed into fresh plowed rows. Her hair was bound in a fat plait and swinging over her shoulder. She was humming, her skirt swishing about her ankles in time as she moved along. She seemed content to do the work of a field hand with no complaint, but it grated on him. He wished to scoop her up and carry her to a veranda where she could sit in a cushioned chair and sip lemonade and enjoy life once again. He had made a vow to himself to make her life easier and, since observing her kindness to his family, he was bound to keep it.

Chapter 5

Sarah let it be known that the reward for finishing the planting would be to attend the first singin' in the county since the war interrupted the social flow. The long-anticipated Saturday dawned clear and cool. She took special care with dressing for the occasion. The hard years had taken a toll on her physically. She stared into the mirror inspecting a complexion that once resembled peaches and cream. Her face was now a golden tan. A carefully trimmed ribbon was cinched around her thin waste to match her six-year-old butter yellow dress. Her hair was caught up under a plain bonnet adorned with a few odd scraps from her mother's notions basket. She did the best she could with what was left of the few lovely things she once had.

"Sarah, time to go," Carrie called up the stairs.

Jacob's gaze followed her down the stairs. Drinking in her changed appearance, she seemed a beam of sunlight after a storm. Golden. He felt ill-groomed in her glow. He followed her out to the drive, his hand just inches behind her waist; his mind resisting his will to touch.

As they approached the wagon, he moved to her side and offered his hand. She looked up in surprise, as if she had long forgotten such attentions. She placed her warm hand in his, he savored the feel of it despite the rough places. Lifting her small form to the box took no effort. He felt a growing need to wrap her in his protection. He knew his thoughts could not continue in this direction. He had no long-term common goals upon which to base such an understanding with her.

As Jacob handed her into the wagon, Sarah noticed that he filled out his crisp white shirt and freshly pressed pants better than when she first saw him, hat in hand, on her front drive. She was pleased that the food and shelter on the farm seemed to have improved his health. His thick dark hair, which usually fell over his brow, tempting her to brush it with her fingertips, was neatly combed. She felt warmth everywhere he touched her.

"I hope Joshua will be there, he is the best leader. He beats out a livelier tune than the others." Carrie interrupted her uncomfortable sensations, reminding her of past gatherings.

She attempted polite conversation as she thumbed through her Sacred Harp Book recalling the familiar tunes as she ran her fingers along the shape-notes.

Of all the social customs of the community, she

especially loved the singin's. Her voice was a gift she learned to use as a young child. Music was the language of God. It lifted her in times of joy and gave her solace in times of sorrow.

Since the war her weariness was so profound, she could not give utterance to the melodies she loved. They now comforted her only in her thoughts or in snippets hummed while she worked. The past few weeks buoyed her hope that all might come out right again. It would never be the same, but God would make it all right according to His will for her.

She could scarcely contain her eagerness to begin the day. She felt the music thrumming up from her soul even before the first note was struck.

∞∞∞

"Carrie, Sarah!" Mary Jane Mullens shouted as they pulled into the churchyard. "Haven't seen you in an age!"

"Well, if we hadn't begged and pleaded, Sarah would have still had us chained to the plow." Gray jumped down and sashayed Mary Jane around in a circle.

"Gray. Gracious, you've grown." Mary Jane laughed as she caught her breath. "Now let go. I'm a little too old for you."

"You never know, I like older women!" Gray waggled his brows at Carrie's best friend.

"Better hurry in, I hear them tunin' up now."

Mary Jane led the group inside the church.

"Now Gray, you are going to stay inside and sing." Sarah knew what Gray had in mind and it wasn't singing. He gave her an insolent look just as his best friend James Blalock raced up and clapped him on the back. They turned the opposite direction of the church door and loped off to find their friends.

All the rough-hewn wooden pews were turned in toward the middle of the room to form a square. The folks were taking their places in their sections. Sarah showed Cordelia to the alto section, the part she claimed when she produced her own Sacred Harp Book. She pointed Charles and Gray to the baritone's seats. She and Carrie sat directly across the room, facing Jacob and Charles.

Joshua Dickens stood across the room taking suggestions for the first round of hymns, thumbing through his book to mark the pages to order them to assure a variety of tempo, texts, and moods.

Then he stepped into the middle of the square and called the class to order. He offered up an opening prayer and then gave the names and page numbers of the first songs to be sung.

"New Harmony, page 406." Mr. Dickens hummed the lead pitch of the first song.

As he struck a pitch from memory, the singers chimed in, each in their proper register. Sarah found her note and proceeded to sing the tune, unaccompanied, with the group in "fasola" style the first time through. Then they sang the verses without accompaniment as they were taught by the Sacred Harp singing school leaders that traveled the Southern circuit for years.

> *"I want to live a Christian here,*
> *I want to die a shouting,*
> *I want to feel my savior near,*
> *While soul and body's parting."*

The singing became more intense with each verse until Sarah was immersed in the emotional force of the music. The church house was perfect for holding the sound and she was thrilled when the chords bounced off the walls and back into the group. As the singing progressed, tears began to flow. Sarah wept when the music became so intense that it expanded and filled the room. Light filtered through the tall windows illuminating the white-washed walls. An aura hovered over the worshippers, evoking the overpowering presence of God. She wept in remembrance of those souls and bodies that had parted—those no longer in the square. When the last chord faded, she looked around to see many drying their eyes. Her gaze lighted on Jacob just as he opened his eyes to return a pain-filled stare directly at her.

Leaders were called one by one to beat out a song of their choice until the singers were exhausted and broke for a picnic lunch before resuming in the afternoon.

"I have never heard better singin'." Carrie plopped down on the blanket-covered ground, her face pink and animated.

"There are some fine singers among the visitors," Mary Jane observed, eyeing the refugees invited by the organizers as a friendly gesture. "Your hired men can hold up the baritones—they are uncommonly good. Are you going to introduce me to them, Sarah?"

"Of course," Sarah replied, noting that Mary Jane finally edged the conversation to her real goal. She was not sure she wanted to subject the men to Fulton's most notorious flirt.

"Here they come, now I expect an introduction," Mary Jane struck as refined a pose as she could on a picnic blanket.

"Brought some chicken, beans, and potato salad." Cordelia motioned the men to place the basket on the ground and gestured toward the church house where a long table held the desserts collected from the singers that morning. "There's desserts over there if you want to take a stroll later."

As the McKennas were seated, Mary Jane elbowed Sarah.

"Mary Jane, I do not believe you have been introduced to the McKennas. Mary Jane Mullens—Cordelia, Jacob, and Charles McKenna."

"Cordelia, Jacob, Charles, what fine voices you have. Did you all have singin's like this in your old home?" Mary Jane gave her hand to each, dipping her chin coyly at the men. She then fixed her eyes on

Charles who, despite his awkward gait, was looking very handsome for the occasion and attracting more than a few glances from the attention starved ladies.

"We did—learned to sing when we were knee-high to a grasshopper." Charles grinned, then bit into a crispy fried chicken thigh.

"Sarah, here, was the only five-year-old ever allowed into the square. She's one of our best singers. The Partins were all our best voices. They carried the class at these get-togethers." Mary Jane chattered.

Sarah knew Mary Jane was oblivious to the pained looks that came, and were quickly hidden, at the mention of the missing family members. Her friend had a habit of speaking without benefit of self-censoring and today would be no exception.

"You will lead 'New Britain' as always at the end, won't you Sarah? No one can lead it like Sarah."

"I will, if asked," she quietly responded, embarrassed by the flattery.

"You will be asked. I will see to it." Mary Jane redirected her attention to continue her interrogation of the McKenna men.

Sarah knew she was using every trick in a flirt's book to engage Charles. She could sense Carrie's agitation at the attention Charles was paying to her friend. It appeared Mary Jane's advances put Carrie on alert. She noticed the growing warmth of the friendship between Charles and Carrie. It was too soon to call it an attachment, but it could lead in that direction, so she was keeping a close eye on the two of them.

"Charles, would you like some dessert?" Carrie

stood to leave.

"I believe I would, I'll come with you," Charles pushed himself up and offered his arm. Sarah noticed the look between the rescuer and the rescued and was afraid she was too late to stop runaway horses already out of the barn.

"So, Miss Partin, you are a particular singer?" Jacob spoke rarely other than to ask about work needing to be done. He toiled relentlessly and took his meals in silence. Sarah was surprised by his inquiry.

"Well some say so but I don't know, all I know is that I love to—I cannot stop myself." Sarah could not look at him directly. She was not accustomed to talking about herself.

"I know." He did not need to say more. She met his gaze. She understood that he did know how the music affected her. She saw it in his face today as he sang, sometimes with his eyes closed as in prayer, sometimes looking directly at her with that intense light in his eyes.

"I will look forward to hearing you sing." Jacob's gaze held hers as he stood. Then he nodded to her, and then his mother, to be excused. She followed his progress as he moved across the yard.

The church bell rang, calling the singers back for the afternoon session. Sarah lead the final hymn. It had been so long. She felt a slight unease to be in the middle once more. She called the song, 'New Britain', and the shuffle of pages indicated all knew the location of this melancholy favorite. She gave the pitch and after she led the vocalization of the tune she stopped and haltingly addressed the crowd, "I'd like to dedicate this, our last song, to all our fallen of Fulton, who I believe we will see again bye and bye." She then led out in a clear soprano voice:

"Amazing grace, how sweet the sound,
That saved a wretch like me
I once was lost but now I'm found,
Was blind, but now I see."

Sarah could feel the Spirit moving as they sang and remembered their losses. She believed God would heal their individual and collective sorrows and give strength for them to still sing His praise. As the last note faded, Mr. Dickens dismissed the crowd that was more subdued than when they began.

∞∞∞

"Has anyone seen Gray?" Sarah turned in a circle surveying the crowd streaming into the yard to the wagons.

"He did not come back to the church after lunch," Carrie said as she loaded their things for the trip home.

"I'll go find him," Jacob offered and headed to the back of the church and the outdoor conveniences. He saw a group of young men congregating there earlier. As he rounded the corner, he heard the exhortations of the crowd of boys huddled in a circle egging on the one in the center. An older player was urging, "Throw the dice kid!"

Jacob clearly understood the scene as he strode into the center and leaned over to speak directly into Gray's ear, "Drop the dice and come with me now and I won't make a further scene to embarrass you."

Gray looked up with shock into the determined man's face. Despite the implied risk to his reputation, he complied. He handed off the dice and eased out of the crowd to growls of disappointment that he would not continue his winning streak against one of the refugee boys. "Sorry fellas, gotta go. James will take my turn."

The insistent young man urging Gray on, stepped up to block the path. "This here your new brother Gray?" he asked with a sneer.

Jacob answered, "No, but I am a friend of his sister and I believe she would have him spend his time more productively. Now if you will excuse us—" Standing his ground, he watched the bully take stock of the clenched fists at his side. Then the tough stepped aside. Jacob nudged Gray along the path toward the front of the church.

"Did you gamble with the money Sarah gave you this week for supplies? You said you lost it while we were in town." Jacob gently gripped Gray's arm and hurried him toward the wagon.

"What's it to you? You're not my brother and can't tell me what to do!" Gray jerked his arm free and surged ahead.

Jacob caught up and replied in a low, warning

tone, "No, I am not your brother but as long as I am on the place I will not let anything or anyone come between your sister and her goal to save the farm. It's for you. So, show some gratitude and stay out of trouble."

"I don't care about the stinking farm. I want to go to Texas with my friends. They're all leavin' but Sarah won't hear reason. The farm is done in, we can't save it," Gray scoffed.

"Not if I can help it," Jacob bit out. "Now hand over the money you got today; it's going back to Sarah."

Gray stopped abruptly and pulled the wad of practically worthless Confederate bills out of his pants pocket and shoved them at Jacob. "That's only so you don't tell."

"I won't, this time, but you need to think about your actions and what it is to lead an honest and honorable life, son. It's more important now than ever," Jacob admonished quietly. He knew that Gray did not understand the meaning of his sermon. He needed good men to show him by example. He resolved to take on the task as long as he was involved with the Partins.

Sarah could feel the tension between Gray and Jacob but could not guess the reason. That evening Jacob produced the bills that Gray had supposedly lost. He offered a story for cover that sounded slightly suspicious to her, but she was relieved to have the money back in hand. It could still be used locally so she let the matter drop.

"You did a good job of leadin' today, Sarah." Cordelia looked up from the shirt she was mending. "You do have an exceptional gift."

"Thank you. I wish you could have heard my mother—she could out-sing us all," Sarah deflected the compliment.

"I doubt she could have done better, am I right boys?" Cordelia continued.

"Exactly so," Charles concurred cheerfully.

"Jake?" Cordelia prodded, to Sarah's dismay.

"I enjoyed it very much, Miss Partin," Jacob agreed without looking up from the repair he was making.

Flustered, Sarah gathered her handwork and announced, "Time for me to get to bed, it's been a long day."

After slipping through the house to see that all was in order she quietly ascended the stairs. As she unraveled the plait from her hair, the now familiar night music drifted into the open window. She was disturbed by the hypnotic strains. She changed to her night shift and climbed into bed. Jacob McKenna's steady gaze intruded upon her thoughts. She wanted to ask him if he was the one playing the haunting melodies that moved her so at night, but she did not want to pry. She threw back the covers and padded to the washstand to douse her face with cool water. The music stopped, replaced by the familiar spring night noises of soft breeze and insect's song. She moved to the window and looked out over the lawn, slowly focusing on the silhouette of her tall hired man leaning against the sturdy oak. She felt a connection to him that she could not understand, and it was growing. She was unable to stop it.

Chapter 6

"The good Lord has surely favored us with a good crop this year," Eli Blalock struck up a conversation with Jacob as he loaded supplies at the feed store. "Weather's been perfect. We've been over to the Neely's pickin' corn and they're comin' to our place the next few days. We'll have some big shuckin's the next few weeks. I expect I'll see your family and the Partins next week at our barbeque?"

"We'll be there. I do appreciate your help gettin' the Partin's crop in and I'll be glad to help with yours." Jacob stopped to wipe his brow on his shirt sleeve, the late June sun blazed down on the men with a vengeance.

"Ya'll still signing on to the train in August?" Eli asked.

"Assumin' we get a fair price for the crops and our share covers expenses. I take it you're still leavin'." Jacob resumed loading the wagon.

"Yup...can't wait to get out to the Bend. My sister's family's already there. She claims it's Heaven on Earth."

"I hope you're right. I could use a change of scenery after the last four years," Jacob commented staring at the ground as the images he hoped for mixed with those recently seen.

"Tell Sarah to bring her pound cake next week, she makes the best in the county." Eli pushed off from the post he was holding up and headed toward the mercantile. "Gotta go regulate the Mrs.' spendin' or I could lose my stake."

Jacob cleared his thoughts and finished the load then pulled the wagon up to the bank to wait for Sarah. He could see she was upset as she exited and allowed him to help her up into the driver's box.

"I cannot believe the audacity of the man," Sarah began an agitated litany of insults that she suffered while speaking to the new bank manager. "First, he asked me to return with my husband and when I told him I had none, he talked to me as if I were a child. I know I could have gotten an extension on our debt from Mr. Sims, but this foreigner has no sensibility for our situation and no mercy!"

"We will make the deadline, Sarah," Jacob's calm voice seemed to soothe her agitation.

"I pray you are right."

"I saw Eli Blalock. He told me to tell you to bring your pound cake to the barbeque, told me it was the best in the county." Jake enjoyed seeing her flush when he repeated the compliment.

"He's just talking, but if the hens bless us with enough eggs, I'll comply." Sarah gave him a rare smile.

"Got the seed to plant the fall crops. We can start tomorrow," Jacob offered.

"You're still leaving in August?" Sarah's smile

faded.

"Yes, I thought I could get you as far along as possible before I do. I'm gonna work up to the day if you'll allow." Jacob looked down on her bowed head and felt a pang of regret that he would leave this vulnerable woman alone. To ascribe more to the feeling would require taking bolder action and he was not at all sure it would be appreciated. Sarah generally kept her emotions in check and her true feelings were often unreadable. He developed an uncanny ability to anticipate her wants pertaining to work and the needs of the farm. To ascertain how she might feel about a penniless refugee paying court, he was afraid to guess.

"I am much obliged to you for offering to help us further. Once I sell the crop, I know your obligation is fulfilled. But if you continue on for a while I will try to help with some provisions for your trip," Sarah countered his offer.

"That won't be necessary, just continuing to shelter us for a time will be enough," he requested.

Jacob handed the carefully wrapped pound cake to Sarah and climbed up beside her. The last harsh rays of mid-day sun gave way to the cooling late afternoon breeze. Families streamed toward the Blalock farm on foot and by wagon. The laughing and merriment had already begun in anticipation of the fun to come. Shuckin' time was in full swing and Sarah enjoyed the social aspects of coming together with the community to do what would otherwise be an onerous chore. Many of the Fulton families were signing on to join the train for Texas. She was unable to imagine the town as it would be without life-long friends to greet her as she walked the streets. She blocked the thought for now. She would face it when the time came.

As she balanced the cake on her knees, the old buck board jostled her into Jacob's side at every dip in the dusty, hard-packed road. Each point of contact needled her body into acknowledging that his was close. It was disturbing. She was becoming increasingly at ease with Jacob over the months since the singin' as they worked together to tend the fields and to renew the farm. He seemed to read her needs intuitively, a phenomenon that she wondered at but didn't study too closely. The growing connection she acknowledged was unsettling. She did not want to get too attached—his goals could not match her own. He planned to move on, she would cling to the family land and legacy. Yet she began to feel a faint dread to face the day they would part.

As they pulled into the Blalock's yard, Gray leaped off the backside of the wagon to run ahead with James. Mattie Blalock was directing the women to the plank table placed between the house and the barn. Every good thing that Southern women could conceive of was displayed on the groaning boards dressed with a riot of colorful, mismatched cloths.

"It's just like old times," Carrie observed with a wide smile on her face.

"At last," Sarah agreed, as she safely delivered the requested cake.

The men gathered at the large square pit to admire the three whole hogs hanging from poles over smoking hickory wood since dawn. They were back-slapping and challenging one another concerning the shuckin' to be done later in the evening. Jacob's mouth watered at the thought of the fine meat that would be served. There had already been a couple of shuckin's but the Blalock's was the most anticipated.

"Long time since I've seen a spread like this, brother. The ladies have out-done themselves." Charles clapped him on the back. "I just heard that the prize for the shucker finishing his pile first will be a Jersey milk cow. Can you believe that? Blalock can't take more than one to Texas so they're givin' the other up. I'm determined to get that cow for Carrie—and Sarah."

Jacob heard the pause before Charles added Sarah's name and knew that Charles was thinking of Carrie particularly. He would have to keep an eye on this growing attachment between Charles and Carrie as it could prove inconvenient when the time came to leave.

"Jacob, glad to see you, but I'm more than glad to see that cake." The huge bear of a man grabbed and pumped his hand, jerking him out of his worried thoughts.

"Couldn't disappoint, Eli."

∞ ∞ ∞

A loud clanging commenced as Mattie banged two pans together to get everyone's attention. "Folks, we are pleased as punch to have ya'll here." The crowd gave out a shout. "We got a mess o' meat and all the fixin's and if I can get that man of mine, wherever he is, to bless it we'll get this party started."

Eli stepped up onto the porch where his wife was pacing like a stage actress and called the crowd to prayer.

"Ya'll bow your heads. Heavenly Father, bless this food we are about to receive to the nourishment of our bodies and make us mindful of the needs of others. We thank you for bringin' our families through the recent conflict. We ask that you comfort those who mourn and restore those who have lost so much. We thank you for this time of fellowship and the bountiful harvest before us. In Jesus' name we pray, Amen."

A chorus of "Amens" put the period at the end of the prayer and one eager youngster shouted, "Let's eat!"   The crowd moved on the tables like stock to the trough, jostling and chattering. It was music to Sarah's ears.

Mary Jane Mullens nudged in beside her. "I see your handsome fellas are here. How's it going out at your place with them there and all."

Sarah knew she would have to deflect Mary

Jane's curiosity at the idea of two single men being encamped at the home of two single ladies. Cordelia, not being their relative, did not count as a proper chaperon. The townspeople knew the hard circumstances that now necessitated odd arrangements and censured no one for doing what they thought they must, but idle talk among the younger set was still a favorite sport.

"We are doing just fine, thanks for inquiring," Sarah answered with a stiff smile as she watched the crowd move down the line piling food on assorted china plates.

"Saw Carrie at the mercantile with Charles the other day. They seem to be gettin' close if my eyes don't deceive me," Mary Jane probed indelicately.

"We come to town together all the time. I don't see why that would indicate anything special," Sarah responded, irritated.

"Well, I saw her picking out some ribbon and she asked his opinion and then guess who paid for it," Mary Jane moved in closer to emphasize the conspiratorial nature of the news she had to offer.

Sarah spied Carrie across the lawn. The new ribbon, she had confessed to buying with part of the supply money, was threaded delicately through her up-swept hair. She turned to look Mary Jane in the eye to receive the already comprehended answer, trying to hide her shock. "Well?"

"Charles!" Mary Jane exulted in being the first to tell Sarah. She did not mean to be cruel. She was just unaware of the harm she caused with her gossip.

"I am sure you are mistaken. Carrie would never act so improperly as to accept such a gift from a man who is not her intended." Sarah was not sure her statement was accurate, but she covered for her sister until she could confront her.

"Ask her then, I am sure of what I saw," Mary Jane responded while waving to another friend. Then she skipped off to tell the tale to all in attendance, Sarah was sure.

As the evening progressed, she was on agitated alert to hear any mention of Carrie's behavior but could not ascertain any.

∞∞∞

When the shuckin' began around nine o'clock Eli whipped the crowd into a frenzy. As the shuckers stepped up, the crowd cheered wildly for all who wished to vie for various prizes. Eli explained that, beside the fine milk cow that would going to the man who finished his pile first, a kiss from the lady of his choice would await all the men finding the pokeberry corn.

"Let the shuckin' commence," Eli shouted as the crowd gathered around the great piles of fresh-picked corn. The shuckers, including Jacob and Charles, were in position. Someone a few paces off fired a gun and the melee began. Husks flew in every direction and the crowd cheered them on. Within moments Charles "hallooed" and jumped up to raise a golden ear, shot through with red kernels that guaranteed a kiss. He hunkered back down, determined to win the grand prize.

"Look, Jake's got one!" an excited refugee cried as Jacob revealed a red flecked ear. He quickly stuffed it in his shirt front hoping to conceal it.

"James, who you gonna kiss?" Gray called over his shucked pile to his friend who held a prized ear high in the air. His cheeks matched the rosy kernels.

The spectacle ended several hours later when Charles jumped up again, threw down his last shuck and ear and shouted, "Done!" The crowd roared. He was pulled from behind his enormous pile and declared the over-all champion. The milk cow was his. The participants were exhausted, but possessors of the pokeberry ears would be expected to honor the tradition of picking a girl to kiss when they were recovered.

With the shucking done, all the newly stripped ears were loaded into the cribs to dry. It was near midnight, but the crowd was just getting started with the pranks and frivolity.

"Get the rail," James shouted, not wanting to spare his father this bit of tradition. Gray helped gather the younger men to snag James' father. They placed Eli atop a fence rail and carried him through the barn door where a well-placed cohort showered him with a pail-full of water as he passed. He was then unceremoniously dumped onto the plank floor that had been set down for the dance to follow. The boys then began to stamp their feet as if stomping ants, the fiddles tuned up, and the dancing commenced.

Jacob slipped to the wagon to get his fiddle and, returning to the barn, he dispatched the worrisome poke ear into the fire pit. He hurried to take his place on the make-shift podium, joining the blended chorus of fiddlers, both town-folks and refugees. It was the first time he had brought his instrument to a Fulton social and his talent for playing the cheerful reels became evident to all. Eli joined the players, once he had a dry shirt, and called the dances. The tempos thrummed to a fevered pitch.

"Jake," a refugee yelled across the clamor between dances, "show 'em what the Sand Mountain boys can do on a fiddle!"

"Hey Blalock, you gonna' let them 'Bama boys talk like that here in Mississip'," a Fulton resident returned in friendly challenge.

The crowd agitated until the two men took the podium for a duel of the fiddles.

Jacob closed his eyes and let it rip. The fast fingering coming as naturally as breathing, he lost himself in the reel finishing with a hard, last swipe over all four strings and thrusting the bow into the air. He opened his eyes as the crowd erupted into shouts and applause. Instinctively, he searched the room for Sarah and locked onto her shining eyes. Her look of approval took his breath away.

Eli cried off a response, keeping Jacob's arm up in the air to indicate victory in this challenge. "Time to have the shuckers claim their prizes," he shouted, grinning at his musical opponent.

∞∞∞

The crowd erupted again and began to call for Jacob's choice of a young lady to kiss. His attempt to fool the crowd had failed. They had not forgotten. Apparently, as prize for winning the musical contest he would go first for a kiss. He began to burn with embarrassment and frustration.

Mary Jane shot Sarah a mischievous grin. Then she began to chant, "Sarah, Sarah!" Soon, the crowd was echoing as they located their prey and began to push her toward the podium.

The now horrified look on Sarah's face was more painful to Jacob than that of a stranger's would have been. He would not embarrass her by rejecting her in front of the crowd, he just prayed she would endure the kiss and they could be done satisfying the mob. She stumbled onto the podium and he caught her arms to brace her. He studied her face, then leaned in to claim his prize. As his lips brushed hers in the slightest imitation of the custom, he felt the ageless spark of recognition, soul to soul, and was shocked in that instant. He backed away, first with wonder at the intensity of feeling surging through him, and then with sadness at the certainty that she could never be his.

Sarah watched with admiration as Jacob's musical

ability was revealed, unmasking him as the nighttime musician of her dreams. She enjoyed watching him play, his passion for the music streamed up from the strings with every stroke. Now the mood turned as the exhausted crowd moved to a new distraction. Sarah was mortified to be singled out. Such a spectacle, at her expense, was not to be endured. She supposed they all thought her past prime, and the current living arrangements at her place excited their imaginations, but to tease her was cruel. She hoped Jacob would not reject her in front of all her acquaintances. As she was pushed into him, she knew by his stern look that he did not wish to kiss her. She was strangely sorry for it as she closed her eyes to receive his attention.

In the instant that Jacob's lips touched hers, Sarah felt the frisson of souls touching and knew from that moment her world had shifted. How would she face him every day and keep her newly acknowledged feelings from being exposed? She backed away, her gaze fixed on the lips that had, in an instant, spun a thread of attachment that might be impossible to break.

The two were pulled apart to allow for James to be pushed to the podium to claim his kiss. He chose his mother for the honor of a peck on the cheek as the crowd applauded his chivalry. Then Charles was called to the front.

"Charles, I'd like to present Belle, our second-best cow, for the honor of bein' the best doggone shucker in Itawamba county. Until the next shuckin' of course." The crowd roared with laughter. Eli was clearly enjoying his part as master of ceremonies. "Now, you also rightfully found a poke ear entitlin' you to a kiss. I'll let you cry off kissin' Belle in favor of the girl of your choice. Who's the lucky young lady?"

The crowd quieted to hear his response.

Charles hesitated a moment as if considering his move and then led Belle through the crowd to stop before a surprised Carrie. "Carrie, I know we talked about waitin' to tell our plans but now just seems right. I'd like to offer this cow as my token of promise and ask you to be my wife."

A buzz of astonishment shot through the crowd, then a hush to hear her answer.

Carrie's gaze darted warily to Sarah standing stiffly across the room then back to Charles. She replied without reserve, "I will Charles, yes, I will!" She stepped into his open arms for the prized kiss.

The crowd erupted, the fiddler's started up a tune and Charles swept Carrie across the floor in triumph. Sarah ran from the room as Jacob watched from the podium, unable to follow without creating further speculation among the revelers. The impression of her lips still warmed his.

Carrie found Sarah outside and quietly slipped up beside her. "We were gonna' tell ya'll soon. I am sorry you had to find out this way."

"It's okay Carrie, I am happy for you both."

"I will hate to leave you and Gray, but I cannot give Charles up, I hope you'll understand."

Sarah had not had time for the realization to sink in that Carrie would leave for Texas with the McKennas. Her sense of grief pressed harder.

"We'll be alright." Of this she was not at all sure. "You are sure about your feelings?"

"I've been sure a long while. I can't explain it, we just knew the minute we met. I know it seems sudden, but I know it is right."

Sarah placed her hands over Carrie's. "Then I am at peace with it and I wish you God's blessing."

The sisters embraced and clung for a while as they began the long goodbye.

"What were you thinking?" Jacob wore a rut in the dust where he was tramping back and forth exercising his agitation. "We are leaving next month. We can't split up the family."

"Don't intend to. I'm addin' to it. Carrie's goin' with us to Texas."

"You fool, I am not talkin' about our family. I'm talkin' about theirs. This loss will kill Sarah. Gray is liable to sneak off and go with the train by himself like he's threatened to do. We can't just go off and leave them alone."

"Well Sarah and Gray just need to come along. The farm is a lost cause," Charles stated the truth as he saw it. "She'll work herself to death to save it and for what? Gray doesn't want it or care."

"You and I both know Sarah will never leave." Jacob agreed with Charles but knew they could not convince Sarah of the harsh facts.

The brothers were interrupted by well-wishers who hoisted Charles up and carried him off to find Carrie for a bit of teasing.

Cordelia eased in beside Jacob at the fence rail.

"I saw it comin', Mama, and I didn't stop it."

"Wasn't your place, son. How do you know this is not God's plan?"

"Would it be God's plan to wound Sarah so?" Jacob bit out.

Cordelia studied her son in the moonlight, then smiled. "God will work it out for us all, son. I am sure of that."

"I will take your word for it—you are more intimate with Him of late than I am," he muttered.

∞ ∞ ∞

The drive home at dawn was marked by uneasy silence. They were all exhausted, body and soul. Clouds were building in the south. The wind was uncharacteristically strong. Jacob hoped the storm would not be extended as there was corn drying and ready to be shucked next week. With fresh scythed wheat to be threshed and hay to cut, the work was never done.

Then new crops needed to be planted. Good weather was required, and this year God had provided. As they pulled into the yard the rain began to pelt the dry dirt, they all scurried to get the wagon unloaded and Jacob drove the stock to the barn.

As he forced the barn door shut against the building wind, he realized with dread that this was no ordinary storm. Most summer storms came down from the northwest, this was pushing hard from the south. He resisted the thought of hurricane, but it would not abate. He thought of the implication of such a storm at this critical harvest season. The crops could be ruined, lost to the delay in processing or to the damp or, worse, flood. He reared back in rising dread and shouted, "God, not now!" Then with the same resignation he had felt when surging across the bleak battlefields into enemy fire, he determinedly pushed through the smaller exit from the barn and ran through the maelstrom to the house. He found the small group gathered around Cordelia as she prayed aloud for God's protection from the trial that they all knew was coming.

Chapter 7

"The lull has come. I'm going out to check the stock." Jacob strode to the door. "Charles go take a look out back, check the west side, see if those trees are down on any buildings. Gray, go latch down the shutters we didn't get to." The men scattered to take advantage of the brief window inside the storm to prepare for the next few hours.

Sarah made her way to the porch to stare up at the wall of clouds swirling around the window to the blue sky above. It was an awesome and terrible sight with the wind stalled to a mere breeze, and all was eerily quiet. She experienced the remnants of hurricanes in Mississippi before, but none matched the force that this one packed, even hundreds of miles in from the coast. She could imagine what destruction must lie to the south. Debris already lay across her land and the back end of the storm was still to come. It would be stronger than the beginning.

"God protect us," Carrie quietly spoke a prayer.

"Let's get some water drawn and see if we can gather some food." Cordelia called as she headed to the cellar to check the stores.

"We need to get all we can in the house in case

it floods." Sarah descended and returned in a steady rotation, grabbing all she could carry to the kitchen to safety.

"Carrie, go check the eggs, get all you can. I'm going to the smokehouse." Sarah ran toward the small building, mud sucking at her boots. The wind was already picking back up. She threw all the meat she could carry, shared from the recent barbeques, into the drawn-up lap of her skirt and started across the yard. Debris began to fly again, pelting her from all sides. Jacob came to meet her and shielded her as they made the porch and the safety of the house.

"What were you thinking," he growled as he pushed the door shut against the wind and turned to glare at her.

"That we might lose the smokehouse and all in it this afternoon," Sarah shot back. "We are going to need all stores we've got to make it through the next few days."

Jacob could not argue that, but the fear he felt when he realized Sarah was still outside when the storm resumed was overwhelming. He steeled himself from such feelings for years, as death and destruction became routine. He had no response that would not give away his thoughts. He stepped around her and moved through the house to the windows yanking shut any curtains left open to shield from the glass not yet shattered.

Sarah made her way to the kitchen to lay out the small pieces of meat she managed to gather. She felt the fear rising as the house began to creak and groan from the force of the wind. She jumped at the random bangs as limbs, and only God knew what, slammed into the defenseless clapboards. She was just grasping the implication of the storm raging outside. All could be lost in one afternoon. Sarah's silent cries welled up into tears as she braced herself against the old table that had been handed down for generations. "God, why? Why now? We are broken already. Are we to be like Job, tormented from all sides? Will I lose all I have today? I cannot bear it! Please God, spare us!"

Cordelia came into the room and wrapped her arms around Sarah's trembling shoulders. "Come into the hallway, it's not safe near all these windows."

The families huddled silently in the hallway, listening to the storm as it assaulted the exterior of the house. When the winds finally died down and just the sound of steady rain beat a lulling rhythm on the roof, they slept in their places on the floor until dawn.

∞∞∞∞

"The water is already rising, I can see it from here." Sarah knew the storm was just the beginning of the trial. Rising flood water from the heavy rains would swallow acres of land, just how much and how high was the question.

"Can we get out across the bridge?" Jacob asked.

"No, I can tell it's already too high. We need to try to get the stock to the hilltop pen. It usually stays above water. The chickens can be brought into the house. We cleared most of the cellar yesterday."

"How long?"

"Half a day, maybe." Sarah looked at him with determination. She would fight till there was no hope left.

"Charles, you and Gray get as much of the corn and hay into the barn loft as you can," Jacob ordered.

The wheat was already gone, soaked and strewn across the fields and with it any hope of a cash sale. What could be saved of the corn and hay would have to go for subsistence of the people and stock, there would not be enough to sell. The water crept closer every hour as they toiled to get the animals, corn, and hay to safety.

The men tramped wearily into the house to find it stripped of all light furnishings. Their chore now was to carry all the heavier furniture to the second floor.

"Here's the last of the food." Sarah handed a large bundle to Cordelia who handed it up to Carrie.

"We've got all the stock up the hill and the loft as full as we can," Jacob reported to Sarah.

"Where's the water's edge?" Sarah asked to ascertain the remaining time until they must climb to the second story and pray the water stopped there.

"It's at the drive and still risin'," Gray answered.

"Everyone make a last sweep of the house. Check for anything left behind and then get on up to the second floor," Sarah commanded.

∞∞∞

"It's still comin'." Gray ran up the top two steps to inform the others that the water filled the entire first floor and was advancing up the staircase toward their refuge. The group huddled among the quickly stowed furniture and light pens filled with squawking chickens. The darkness was illuminated with only two candles in order to conserve the small store for the days ahead when they would be trapped. Sarah racked her mind for the sin she must have committed to plunge her into this hell. The smell of the putrid water inching toward them stung the back of her throat, the heat and humidity was smothering. She looked around at her mates, they seemed to have lost all pretense of hope. Resignation to the will of the Creator to have them live or die was all that was left. She dozed, too exhausted to keep watch any longer.

Water lapped gently at her hem in a sinister tease as it crept to swallow her up. The wet sensation urged her awake to see the danger and she alerted the others.

"Wake up, everyone, get up! Get to the attic!" The others roused to scramble toward the final staircase to the attic carrying anything that was salvageable.

Carrie began to cry softly as Charles urged her forward. Cordelia and Gray gathered assorted food bundles and candles and pushed up the narrow flight to the upper floor. Sarah scrambled to find her most prized possession, the old Bible that held the names of the generations of Partins. She frantically rummaged through the hastily stored piles from below trying to remember where she left the precious bundle of her treasures, wrapped in Mama's favorite shawl.

"Sarah, come on." Jacob held the last lit candle in his hand.

"I have to find my things." Sarah sloshed from one corner of the dark room to the other moving aside unwanted parcels impeding her way.

"What do they look like?"

"They are in a blue shawl."

They slogged around one another, Jacob holding up the dim light.

"Here it is." Sarah snatched the parcel and headed to the staircase. She stopped; suddenly aware the chickens were still sitting in their pens on the tables.

"Jacob, the chickens!" she shouted.

"Have to leave them, pens won't fit up the stairs and we don't have time to carry them." Jacob came up behind her and pushed her up the passageway into the room above.

She turned to face him as he climbed into the room and secured the door.

"I opened the latches and raised a window; hopefully they will find their way out." Jacob tried to soothe her distress while knowing that the likelihood that the fowl could survive was small. They listened to the excited squawking below until silence settled the question as to the fate of the trapped birds. In the coming hours would theirs be the same?

As another morning dawned the water began to recede. It was another day before they could get to the first floor and another before they could set foot on land as the families of Noah, praising God for their lives.

$$\infty \infty \infty$$

"What the wind didn't take, the water did." Jacob stopped shoveling mud from the house to mop his face. He spent the past weeks cleaning up the barn, rounding up the stock and repairing the most desperate damage. Now he would concentrate on the house. It would be a monumental chore to make it livable again. They were all in hastily erected tents now.

"We've got no choice but to keep diggin', Charles. We've got to get things back to normal as possible for them." Jacob could not continue his thought —*before we leave*.

"Everyone in town is alright but most lost their crops and some stock," Gray came riding up on the mule shouting news.

"Water still high at the bridge?" Jacob stopped and came to sit at the edge of the porch steps.

"Yep, but not as fast-movin'." Gray headed toward the shade trees where the women were busy washing linens. "They're formin' up the train for Texas," he yelled back as he crossed the lawn.

Charles plopped down beside Jacob.

"I was afraid of that. With all the folks hurting from the storm I figured they would just decide to go on and leave instead of waiting till September." Jacob stared out across the debris littered field.

"Well what does that mean for us?"

"Means we have to go before we are ready, before they are ready," he nodded toward the ladies.

"How are we gonna' get the supplies with no cash?"

"We are going to have to just go as we are and pray God provides along the way, like with the children in the wilderness," Jacob offered skeptically but sure of his conviction that they must go now.

"Alright, brother, for better or worse, I'm in." Charles looked in the direction of the women and stood. "I best go tell my beloved to get packin'."

Jacob was not ready to tell Sarah. He did not know how to abandon the wounded. He had not done it in the war and could not stomach the thought now.

"Carrie, we're bound for Texas!" Charles swept his love from her stooped position over the washtub, swinging her into the air and around. "They're formin' the train early!"

Sarah froze in the scrubbing motion and stared at the two frolicking across the grass. She slowly digested the dreaded news. They were leaving her— early. She turned and walked out into the littered field. She squeezed the moisture from her eyes with determination. She would send Carrie off without guilt.

"Sarah, you heard the news?" Carrie skipped up beside her. "The train is leavin' early. You will come with us. You must."

"I cannot go. There's nothing for me there. Gray and I need to stay and keep the land Mama and Daddy worked so hard to secure. I'm a single woman. I cannot go out to Texas alone and survive and I don't want to be an extra in your house. Surely you understand." She turned to embrace her sister, "But you must go without reserve. Your life is with Charles now once you two are wed."

Carrie pushed her back at arms-length, "We'll just see about that. I am determined not to leave without you."

"Well then you have a hard row to hoe, because my mind is made up in this matter." Sarah smiled, hiding the unease she felt building.

∞∞∞

The evening breeze relieved the suffocating heat only slightly as they ate the meager supper Cordelia prepared. Charles took his leave to the men's tent and Jacob followed.

"The train is leavin' in two weeks," Charles offered the news he had gotten from Gray. "We'll need to get our wagon in shape, needs some repairs." He waited for a reply and got none. "You're mighty quiet this evening, what's on your mind?"

"You know what's on my mind, I can't feel easy about leaving Sarah and Gray. They're defenseless and it's gonna get worse around here with reconstruction. Yankee interlopers coming down, don't know beans from wild honey about the way we do things. Sarah's strong and smart but she can't out-argue a liar and a cheat. She is used to fair dealing and there won't be anything fair about what's going to happen here. Retribution is what they want, and they will plow under those who stand in their way."

Silence hung in the air as they prepared to bed down. When the light was gone, Charles spoke into the dark. "You could marry her."

The silence expanded as he waited for a reply.

"Now you *are* dreaming," finally Jacob acknowledged the impossible idea. "She's never gonna give up her home and besides she wouldn't want a penniless refugee carrying her off to the wilderness without a stitch to live on."

"You don't know unless you ask her. I didn't think Carrie would have a cripple, but she overlooked it, to my surprise. Sarah is a good woman and will make a fine wife. You may not find such again."

"That's different, you love Carrie and she returns the sentiment."

"I still say you ought to put the question to her."

Jacob could hear Charles settling down to sleep and soon his light snore filled the silence. Knowing he could not sleep now, he crept out into the moonlight.

As he passed the nearby oak, Cordelia softly hailed him, "Couldn't sleep either, son?"

"No." Jacob folded his legs and sat beside her against the trunk.

"Somethin' on your mind?"

"The train pulling out early. I'm not ready to leave but I guess we'll have to go along if we want to stay with the group."

"Just as soon as later, I guess." Cordelia sensed why he hesitated. "This is about Sarah, isn't it."

"It is." Jacob admitted, surprised he was so easily read. "She and Gray can't stay here alone. It's not practical, or safe."

"Are you sure there's not more to it?"

"Meaning what?"

"You know what I'm sayin', son. You don't hide your feelin's very well, at least from your Mama."

"I still don't get your meaning. I like the Partins, don't want to see them hurt."

"Then I'll tell you straight, I think you are becoming attached to Sarah and just don't or won't see it. Your concern is out of proportion to the lack of attachment you claim."

Jacob snorted at the ridiculous idea. "And if it's true, what am I supposed to do, ask her to bind herself to a beat-up soldier without two coins to rub together and leave her home and land to scratch out a living on the frontier?"

"Yes." Cordelia shot back. "Because I think she feels the same toward you."

"Mama, you are a romantic fool." Jacob was exasperated at the turn the conversation had taken.

"Promise you'll give it some thought?" Cordelia

nudged.

"I am sure you will agitate the idea enough for us both." Jacob pushed up and stomped toward the creek.

As he wandered the property through the night, surveying damage on all sides, he knew that there was no way to get the place cleaned up and in sufficient repair in time to leave it to Sarah and Gray to carry on with any hope of success. His Mama might be a romantic, but she was also practical. She could be counted on to voice what was true. Could his Mama be right about Sarah's feelings toward him? If so, could he convince Sarah of the hopelessness of her dream and have her substitute a new one instead?

Chapter 8

Sunlight streamed into the window illuminating her work as Sarah adjusted the delicate lace along the collar of Carrie's best dress. She worked to make the tiny remnant from their mother's wedding dress fit the plain rose-colored garment to add a special touch for the upcoming ceremony. She saved the bits of ivory tatting in hopes of using it on her own wedding dress someday. Now it would be her gift to Carrie. The reality that Carrie and the McKennas would soon be leaving began to weigh heavily on her thoughts. She was afraid—afraid of parting with Carrie and never seeing her again—afraid of the responsibility of the upkeep of the farm once again falling onto her with even less chance of success. She was more afraid that she would not be able to hide her anguish as she felt the sinew, which was binding her daily closer to Jacob, snap when he rode out of her life forever.

"Sarah?"

Sarah quickly stuffed the lace into her bodice as Carrie came into the parlor.

"I was looking for my dress. I see you have it, and why?" Carrie teased.

"Just checking to see if it needed any mending."

Sarah scrutinized the delicate fabric to cover her story.

"And what is this I spy?" Carrie reached over Sarah's lap to snag the edge of hastily stashed lace from its hiding place. Her eyes grew wide as she realized what she held. "Oh, Sarah, you were not adding this to my dress."

"I was and will continue if you will hand it over." Sarah reached for the cream-colored treasure.

"But you were saving this for your own wedding dress." Carrie handed the lacy bit back gently, searching her sister's eyes for confirmation of her claim.

"Well, as we both know I will not likely need it. I decided Mama would want one of us to use it. I could not be happier to give it as my gift to you."

Carrie sat and clasped her sister's hands. "I cannot take it. I know you will need it someday."

"Don't be silly. I insist. Besides, who will be left in Fulton to marry once the train leaves." Sarah disengaged her hands and resumed her measuring to cover her discomfort with the direction of the conversation.

"That's why you must come with us, you and Gray. Charles says the land in Texas is plentiful and rich for farming. We could start over."

"Carrie, a lone woman and a boy cannot embark on such an endeavor."

Carrie cocked her head and with a mischievous smile offered her solution. "You could marry Jacob."

Sarah's hands stilled as she considered Carrie's wishful suggestion. She recalled the soft touch of Jacob's lips on hers and the look of distaste he had tried so hard to cover. Her heart contracted in her chest to think of it. "No, he has shown no inclination toward me and I could not marry a man just to secure a protector."

"But what of Gray, Sarah? He wants to come with us but cannot if you stay. There is little left here to hold him. He does not remember better times. He deserves a fresh start. The revival of this farm is your dream, not his. Surely you see that."

Sarah bowed her head and nodded in agreement. She did know that Carrie was right but convinced herself that she knew what was best for Gray and would pursue it with all her strength. But now her strength was waning. She was adrift in uncharted water struggling into an uncertain future. She could not entertain the lifeline being offered.

"Will you just consider coming along?" Carrie again covered her sister's trembling hands in a warm clasp. "Let God work out the details."

"I will give it careful thought, but I don't see a solution. God will have to work it out."

Carrie gave her hands a squeeze, then rose and left the room.

Sarah finished the last stitch on the collar of Carrie's dress and held it up to admire the effect. The lace was perfect—the dress transformed. She stood, lost in thoughts of her sister's coming wedding, and drifted toward the mirror to hold the dress close to her chest letting it fall full length in a golden beam of light. She began to sway thinking of the music and dancing that would surely be a part of the celebration. As she slowly took a turn around, head down to note the flow of the skirt, she heard the familiar deep voice.

"Suits you."

Her eyes met the steely gaze fixed on her. Crimson stain brushed her pale cheeks. Embarrassed to be caught in such a fanciful moment Sarah turned, rushed out the opposite door, and barreled up the stairs to make her escape.

Jacob pried himself from the door-jam, where he eavesdropped on Sarah in her private reverie, and made his way to the kitchen. He was sure he had never seen a more beautiful sight as Sarah, swaying in time to a private muse, in an aura of late afternoon light filtering through the window.

"What's got Sarah on the run?" Cordelia inquired with an amused grin as she prepared the evening meal.

"Don't know." Jacob moved to the window, making a pretense of checking the weather.

"How's the work on the wagon coming along?" Cordelia clanged the lid back onto the pot of boiling soup stock.

"Good. We should be ready with time to spare." Even the aroma of the makings of his Mother's fine stew could not summon an appetite in his present state.

"Give any more thought to our conversation?"

"Which conversation would that be?" Jacob

knew very well but hoped to skirt the issue.

"The one where I suggest you ask Sarah to come along." Cordelia gave him a determined look.

"I said I'd think on it and I will, but don't push Mother. Your notion is romantic, but this is not a fairy tale." Jacob knew his tone was too harsh, but he was frustrated with his lack of control over emotions he was unfamiliar with. Sarah had a way of knocking him off balance and he was used to taking charge in difficult situations.

"Well you better make your move soon. Sarah deserves some time to think on it too and time is somethin' we are short on." Cordelia bent to her work cutting the stew vegetables and Jacob knew he had been dismissed.

∞∞∞

The evening meal was a strained affair. Sarah and Jacob were silent as the rest of the family tried, in vain, to hold up the conversation. Jacob had lost all enthusiasm for the coming trip. He was consumed with worry for Sarah and Gray. They were in danger due to the precarious conditions under the Yankee occupation. The physical havoc caused by the recent storm added insult to injury. Gray was unhappy and Sarah was not yet aware of his drift toward bad company. He needed a strong male influence to keep him reigned in the right direction.

Yet he could not stay. His own family needed

his strong back if they were to make a go of it on the frontier. Jacob stared at the top of Sarah's bowed head all evening struggling with how he might put a proposition to her and not offend.

Talk of the coming trip slashed at Sarah's increasingly fragile courage to face the change being forced on her. The remnants of her family were being torn from her. Jacob was leaving her behind. The pain was physical and worsening each day as the departure date neared.

Carrie's wedding was planned for the weekend before leaving. Just one week away. How could she keep a smile on her face for Carrie when her heart was breaking?

The intensity of Jacob's glare made her flush every time they met. Then twirling with her sister's dress like a flighty school-girl—she was mortified at being caught so unguarded. He always had a way of catching her at her worst, in dirty field clothes, up to her hips in muddy water, twirling like a child, being pushed into his unwilling arms for a kiss he did not want to give—strong arms she wished to run to for comfort and safety.

"If you will all excuse me?" Sarah pushed back from the table and made her escape out the kitchen door into the cool evening breeze. Making her way to the creek, she bent to splash the clear water onto her face. Slumping back onto the ground she leaned into the old willow tree that had been the boys' fort in better times.

"May I join you?" Jacob came up quietly behind her.

"Yes." Sarah continued to stare into the current breaking around the rocks, like her heart— separating from those she loved.

He sat down beside her, and they watched the flow in silence for a time. Usually surrounded by other family members; his proximity, in her private space, disturbed her. She could hear his breathing, feel his nearness without a touch.

"Sarah, you know we are leaving soon." His deep voice startled her.

"Yes." She became more uneasy as she sensed his hesitation.

"I cannot feel comfortable leaving you and Gray alone."

"We will be alright. We have managed before and will again," Sarah said, with manufactured conviction, still staring into the slow flowing water. "It is not your concern to worry about us, you have your family counting on you and that is enough to carry."

"Sarah, look at me."

Noting the unusual tone of command in his request, Sarah looked into his eyes and found herself mirrored there. She studied his face to memorize it for the lonely years to come.

Jacob felt the caress of her gaze as if she were physically touching his features and was almost undone and then knew his next words were right and true and his heart's desire.

"Sarah, I would like for you to come with us—with me." He stumbled to go on hoping he could convince her without frightening her. He could be mistaken in his reading of her intense gaze. "Gray too, of course."

"Jacob, you know I cannot. Gray and I cannot fend for ourselves alone in an unfamiliar setting. I will not be a burden to your family."

He pressed on before he could lose his nerve. "Sarah, you misunderstand. I am asking you to come as my wife. I need a strong woman by my side, and you are the strongest I've ever known. And I would be honored to be your protector. It need be nothing more than that if that is your wish." He tried to read her expression—surprise, shock, rejection?

"Jacob," he covered her words with his hand. She froze under his gentle touch on her lips.

"Just think about it."

He rose, his eyes locked on hers in a silent plea. Then he walked away.

∞∞∞

Over the next few days Jacob, Charles and Gray worked to ready the wagons for the coming trip. Sarah, Carrie and Cordelia packed the provisions for home and hearth. Sarah considered Jacob's offer.

He had left her weak, from longing for his arms to wrap her in the safety that his offer implied.

She knew in her heart of hearts that the farm was past redeeming. Acknowledging this, she still rebelled against the idea of such an arrangement of convenience. Even though such marriages were not uncommon, she had always hoped for her husband's love in her marriage. He had offered his protection, not affection. But despite his lack of a declaration of love, she knew that she loved Jacob and needed to be with him. Could she marry him in an act of practicality and live close by his side and not let her true feelings overwhelm and expose her to his rejection?

Sarah tried to avoid closer proximity to Jacob as they gathered and packed their belongings, but as they sat for meals his intense stare was unavoidable. Any time he came near she could sense his spirit compelling her to step into the unknown with him.

On the third evening after his declaration, her nerves were drawn tight as a bow string. She knew she must give an answer soon. Then she heard the wistful strains of Jacob's playing on the night air. The tune was familiar after many nights of repetition and as dear to her as the player. It drew her thoughts to his proposal, and she knew her answer.

Jacob played the melody he had perfected in his late-night thoughts on his muse...Sarah. It was quiet and sweet but with an underlying strength. He could not know if his feeble addresses would win her, but he knew he could not leave her. He had intently watched her work the past few days, fiercely willing her to come to him with an affirmative answer to his proposal. His playing grew more frenzied as his thoughts turned dark. He would convince her and if he could not, he might have to draw on the old saga of the Sabine Women and take her along by force. He stopped abruptly, realizing the uncivilized measure he was contemplating.

"I'll go."

Jacob turned to see Sarah standing disheveled in the moonlight. She looked like a saving angel to him, her curls flying about her head. It took all his strength not to go to her and embrace her as he so longed to do. How he would keep his distance as they lived together, he could not imagine. He knew the proposed arrangement would require it. It would be her choice to amend it.

"Are you sure?"

"I am sure."

Chapter 9

Cordelia and Carrie were overjoyed at Sarah's acceptance of Jacob's offer. Charles was sure he carried off the match all by himself. Sarah and Jacob avoided one another, keeping busy with the necessary work of sorting and loading the accumulation of six people's lives into two large wagons. It was a whirlwind of preparation, provisioning for the trip and preparing for two weddings instead of one. Hard decisions had to be made over what necessities could be compromised for which treasures.

Sarah stole through the house, memorizing the things she cherished that must be left behind. Her gaze fell on the flood-damaged grandfather clock in the hall that had marked all the hours of her life to now, the tiny floral pattern on the muddied curtains in the parlor that Mother had lovingly sewn, the old rocker replaced beside the hearth. She had hoped to use it to lull her own babies to sleep while humming the old melodies; the passed down accompaniments to the lives of generations of Partins that had gone before. The echoes of her brothers' laughter as they scuffled and pranked haunted her. Here were the visuals to remind her not to forget. Once they were out of sight would her memories fade?

"It is hard to part with the things that you love." Cordelia came to Sarah's side at the mantel.

"Harder than I imagined." Sarah fingered the delicate figurine that would never survive the rough ride ahead.

"I realized after I lost my home and all my treasures that all I really cared about was in the wagon with me, my family." Cordelia wrapped her arm around Sarah's waist. "And now I've gained two daughters and another son. I am so blessed."

Sarah smiled at the thought that Cordelia felt so about her family.

"Sarah, I know you are unsure about how you and Jacob will get on, but I want you to trust that all will be well. You both are good and kind, hard-working and constant. That is what it takes to build a strong family. You will not regret your decision. My prayers will be with you and I know God will not fail me as I pray for the love that I know you feel for each other to grow strong and full."

"Oh, Cordelia, am I so transparent?" Sarah turned to her soon to be mother-in-law in anxious surprise.

"I fear so my dear, as is my son," Cordelia laughed.

"I don't believe so, he has never indicated such to me." Sarah shook her head in disbelief.

"He did ask you to marry him."

"To appease his guilt over leaving us behind and to satisfy Carrie and Charles I am sure."

"Well time will tell. Then I will say I told you so. You better go get ready. The whole county is headed this way to see you wed." Cordelia shooed her to the staircase.

It did seem that the entire county was streaming up the drive on foot, by raw buckboard, and in refined carriage. Sarah let the curtain drop and turned back to the mirror for last inspection. She felt somewhat a fraud, unlike Carrie who was openly radiant in her joy. Would her friends and neighbors guess the convenient nature of her agreement with Jacob? Would her eyes give away her own bittersweet happiness that she would not lose him, as she feared, but be forever constrained in her ability to express her feelings?

She did feel she looked her best considering the situation. Her blue plaid dress with ruffled bodice was her best. Her usually flyaway curls were tamed with wild summer blooms tucked in along a trail of narrow blue ribbon wound throughout her hair. She tucked a tiny remnant of her mother's lace, left from trimming Carrie's lovely pink gown, into her chemise close to her heart. Perhaps it would protect that tender organ from pain, strengthening it for the hard years she feared were ahead.

"It's time." Carrie peeked her head into the door. "Sister, you are a vision," she breathed as she came into the room reaching for Sarah's hands.

"As are you," Sarah clasped her sister's hands.

"I am nervous—all those people." Carrie indicated the crowd gathered before the front porch where the ceremony would take place. The church in town and the house were still not in any condition for visitors.

"No need to be, they are all our friends here to wish us well," Sarah reassured but felt the same unease, not being used to such attention.

Cordelia swooshed in with maternal authority in a full skirted gown that had been hidden in her trunk. "Girls, it's time to claim my sons and rid me of the responsibility." She gave each of her future daughters-in-law a welcoming kiss and shooed them out of the room and down the staircase to the front door.

Several fiddlers played the strains of a wedding march. The click of the men's boots as they came onto the porch in front of the door indicated it was too late to renege on promises made. Cordelia opened the door and gently waved first Carrie then Sarah out to meet their mates.

Mary Jane stepped up beside Carrie and Sarah. Gray fidgeted uneasily beside Jacob and Charles. The music faded and the ceremony began.

Jacob reached for Sarah's hand, his gaze sweeping over her in a tender caress. She was a vision of simple beauty. He could not believe he was being gifted with such a partner. As he clutched her work-roughed hand he pledged to himself and to God, as he repeated the formal vows before the preacher and all the congregants, that he would do whatever in his power to one day see them soft enough to caress a baby's cheek. The vision of her in that Madonna's pose loomed and he wrestled the realization that babies might not be part of their bargain. Still he vowed to make her glad of her choice to come with him.

Sarah felt the strength of Jacob's grip pulling her into his side, tucking her in protectively, as his other arm circled her waist. It was an intimacy he had never extended before, warm and reassuring. Then she was lost in the giving and taking of vows meant to last a lifetime. Her "I do" was a soft sigh of surrender and relief and thanks to God for this man beside her. She vowed as she turned to face him for the final blessing that he would be glad of his request that she come with him.

"Gentlemen, you may kiss your brides!" Reverend Jackson announced triumphantly. Charles dipped Carrie into a back-breaking embrace to the loud cheers of the crowd.

Jacob gently pulled her full into himself and quietly, but thoroughly, kissed her. It seemed a solemn promise of more to come if their mutual respect should blossom into stronger emotions in the future.

"Break it up you two," Charles startled the newlyweds who were lost in the intoxicating sensations of their first real kiss.

The fiddlers broke into a fast-paced jig and the celebration began. The men rushed up to pump the hands and slap the backs of the shackled. The women swarmed the brides to kiss their cheeks and compliment their dresses, hair, and tight nosegays of fresh field flowers.

Sarah and Jacob were not able to speak a private word all evening and then it was the last dance saved for the pairs just married. Jacob again pulled her close and as the music lulled them into the rhythm of the dance, the world fell away. They swirled and swayed as one, communing with their bodies that an unspoken bond had somehow been forged. The crowd stilled to silence to watch the pairs glide under the stars. Old couples and young were caught in the romance of the moment, finally joining them in the dance.

When the last guests had gone, Jacob led Sarah to his tent. Her trunks were packed and loaded for the trip to begin the next day. As agreed, two cots were set up onopposite sides of the tent for their first night together and her nightclothes were laid out on one.

"I'm going for a walk, give you some time to get ready for bed," Jacob offered.

"Thank-you," Sarah answered quietly, feeling suddenly shy. When he was gone, she changed to her best nightdress, let down her hair and settled under the light summer quilt.

Her thoughts wandered to the story of the wedding day of the biblical couple Isaac and Rebekah.

They were unknown to one another. They also shared a tent. Their wedding night was demurely described but she knew what happened between them that night. Sarah was shocked to admit that she wished, at that moment, for a more conventional ending to her wedding day. She would welcome Jacob to come to her, to hold her, to complete their vows in the age-old way. But would he? She drifted to sleep with her fingers on her lips recalling the kiss he had given her as he took her to be his bride.

Jacob returned from his walk, and a dip in the creek, taken to redirect his thoughts. He was careful not to wake Sarah as she slept, her glorious hair splayed across the specially embellished bridal pillowcase that looked sadly overdone for the rude cot she slept on. As he lay down on his own uncomfortable berth, he reached out to touch a loose strand and marveled at the silky feel of it.

He realized that he was remarkably innocent for a man his age. His main dealings with women before the war had been those of a young man flirting close to a flame but not yet touching it. He had scrupulously avoided the camp followers during the conflict knowing all too well the sad outcome inflicted on the partakers.

The past year had involved an exhausting trek home and then on, westward, toward an unknown future. He also knew that his feelings for his first love had been nothing compared to the overwhelming need he felt for this woman now beside him. Her price was far beyond rubies. Could he ever be worthy? He fell into fitful sleep with the golden curl still wrapped around his finger.

$$\infty\infty\infty\infty$$

Sarah roused to the groans growing ever more intense and anguished, then finally bursting from her new husband's lips as curses.

"Damned butchers! Come back you cowards!" Jacob was thrashing at the air over his cot. He was frantically trying to push something from him. "God help me!"

Sarah quickly yanked the hair, tangled in his hand, free and tried to wake him. As she reached for him, he fought her, landing a hard blow to her arm.

"Jacob, wake up. You are safe." She continued to try to wrestle him, but his agitation was too great for her to reach him with physical strength.

As a last resort, she began to sing an old lullaby her mother had sung to Gray. It seemed to penetrate the night terror and Jacob calmed. Finally, he quieted as she sat on his cot and cradled his head to her heart. It was not exactly the caress she had imagined but she was satisfied to have him in her arms at last.

Jacob awoke to find Sarah atop him in a tangle of hair and limb. He was mortified that perhaps he had not kept his promise, implied in their agreement, to keep his distance. As he tried to extricate himself, she sleepily came awake. With a squeak of surprised embarrassment, she scuttled off him onto her knees on the floor.

"Jacob, I am sorry, I didn't mean to . . ."

"No Sarah, forgive me. I did not bother you in the night, did I?"

"Well, you did have a bad dream. I tried to wake you but could not."

"Forgive me then. Charles tells me I talk in my sleep. I am sorry I woke you." He reached for her hand to help her up and noticed the large bruise on her upper arm. "Did I do that?" he nodded to the blackish-purple stain.

"I am afraid you did in your battle with the phantoms." Sarah took his hand and rose, a forgiving smile played on her lips.

Jacob flustered at seeing her standing there in her nightdress in broad daylight, all tousled from her sleep.

"If you will excuse me, I will go wash up." He abruptly turned and exited from the temptation. He needed another dousing.

When he returned, Sarah was dressed in work clothes befitting the hard day ahead, her hair bound close to her head in a tight bun and covered with a large sun-blocking bonnet. Temptation averted.

The wagons were packed to the brim with all the necessities and as many treasures as the left-over space would allow. The men packed the tents and harnessed the plough horses that would pull the wagons to town where they would be exchanged for the purchased oxen. In a silent goodbye, Sarah and Carrie made one last sweep of the house, slowly walking through each room touching the floral-patterned walls, Mama's hand-sewn curtains, and door facings where the boys' heights were marked.

Later, as the teams pulled away and across the bridge, Sarah looked back for as long as the view was unobstructed, then turned with determination to face her new life.

∞∞∞

The town square was crowded with wagons and excited pilgrims. The men were summoned to a government meeting where the group finalized the slate of nominated leaders to be in charge of the many delegated duties that would be required to move a train of 30 wagons and 200 people over a thousand miles. The ladies mulled about the wagons, checking the tie-downs one last time.

"Sarah, Carrie," Mary Jane yelled from across the square as she trotted over to the McKenna's wagons.

"Mary Jane?" Carrie greeted her friend with a grin and a hug. "Come to see us off?"

"Why, no. As a matter of fact, I came to tell you

the good news. I am going with you." Mary Jane held up her left hand for all to see the gleaming gold band. "I am now Mrs. Ben Granger," she giggled.

"How? When?" Carrie asked in surprise.

"Just this morning. Had to get the Justice to marry us," Mary Jane explained.

"I didn't know you were seeing the black-smith," Sarah remarked.

"Well, it was kind of sudden. While we were dancing last night, he said he had admired me all along and decided to take a chance and see if I would go to Texas with him." Mary Jane sobered a bit as she spoke, "I have no prospects here, so I agreed. I think you know what I mean, Sarah."

The thrust of Mary Jane's sharp tongue took Sarah by surprise as usual. A blush of embarrassment swept over her as she realized that at least one traveler guessed the nature of her arrangement with Jacob and that one was likely to needle her with the knowledge. Before she could formulate a response, Granger called for his wife. After proper congratulations, he escorted Mary Jane back across the square.

The McKenna men returned from the meeting with news.

"Jacob's been named second in command to Eli Blalock as Captain," Charles announced.

"What does that position involve?" Sarah inquired as she returned to checking her packing for security.

"Well, Eli will be in command. He has made the trip several times to see his sister and he knows the roads. He will direct all navigation and have the final say over all decisions brought before the committee," Jacob explained.

"The committee is the group of men elected today," Charles continued the lesson. "Jacob's job is kinda like that of sheriff. He will deal with any law-breaking or disputes about the rules we vote on at the meetin's."

"Sounds like a lot of responsibility." Sarah mused at the thought that Jacob had earned such respect from her townsfolk in such a short time.

Charles grinned. "It is, but believe me, Jake is up to it. And he will have help, as I am to be his second."

"A kiss for the deputy." Carrie wrapped her arms around Charles in an uninhibited public display of affection and several by-standers gave a whistle.

Soon all was ready, and the families received the starting line-up for the order of the wagons for the first day of travel.

The final good-byes began, and tears flowed as the group embraced old friends and family for what might be the last time.

Eli called the group to quiet. "Shall we pray for safe journey before we set out?"

Over the bowed heads, Eli blessed the travelers and those they would leave behind. "Time to go folks. We will all meet again, with God's grace, either on this side of the River or the other." They dispersed quietly with that solemn assurance and made their way to their teams and waited the order to pull out.

A young refugee, designated the trumpeter to

signal movements of the train, sounded the signal for forward and Eli commanded in a shout, "Let's roll this train!"

A great answering roar went out from the company and the teams began to peel out of the square in the arranged order.

As they got under way Jacob expertly guided the new ox-team to pull in behind Eli as they began in rank order of the government members for the first day. Sarah grabbed her bonnet. and the seat, as the jerking sway of the wagon rocked her hard into Jacob's side. He cocked his head and smiled. Her breath hitched and she looked away to the passing countryside. Realization flooded her once again, she was leaving her life's home to follow her new husband to an unknown land and future. She thought of Rebekah leaving her home for Isaac's and peace settled over her. God would provide all the strength, endurance, and even love she would need to make it work for good.

She turned back to Jacob and observed his command of the team. She studied his hands as he wrangled the wagon forward. They were smooth and tanned, hairless, but not feminine. The reigns were laced between long, slender fingers that, with just a flicker, could bend the will of the thousands of pounds ox team. The animals seemed to sense what she and the people of the party did, that this man was to lead, they were to follow.

Chapter 10

The August sun beat down on the travelers, heat lay-ing on them, smothering and sticky. Even the flies forgot to mount their winged assault. Sarah walked beside the wagon with a scraggly dog trotting closely behind. He attached himself to the train along the way and to Sarah in particular. She offered the starv-ing creature crumbs against advice. She eventually named him Runwell, after an old coon hound her brother Henry had when she was a child. Somehow it gave her comfort to try to save him. The land they were passing through was ravaged almost beyond saving and she imagined he was probably someone's cherished hunter.

"Terrible sight isn't it?" Carrie caught up to her, gesturing out toward the burned farm and cropland they were passing.

"It is and the sad thing is you can't tell who the villains were, Yankees or our own boys." Sarah wiped a trickle of moisture from her brow.

Eli came galloping by shouting a stopping point just ahead of the next water crossing. Charles tipped his hat and jumped from the lazy board on the side of his wagon to walk the rest of the way in order to have better control of the jerk line as the oxen came nearer to the slow-flowing tributary. Jacob did the same up ahead as Gray walked along-side the oxen cracking his whip over the animal's heads to keep them on course. The synchronization of men and beasts looked like a dance to Sarah. All knew their parts and performed them.

Soon the women took up their set as they prepared similar noon meals in similar fashion. Carrie spread the blankets and Cordelia produced a tin of leftover corn cakes from breakfast. Sarah filled tin cups with cool water to wash them down. No fire or cooking was required. Gray let the oxen loose to graze and drink. Soon most of the people, including Jacob and Charles were catnapping, gathering strength for the long afternoon ahead.

"Well Hades could not be hotter!" Charles plopped down beside Carrie who chided him with just a look. "But I won't risk it," he continued, to reassure her. She dimpled prettily and he pecked her, despite the moist sheen on her cheek.

Sarah smiled wistfully at the playful inter-action. Jacob was still most formal with her and she longed for him to be more at ease. Each day they tended to their different tasks, touching only inciden-tally. At night, they fell onto their separate cots, too exhausted for conversation.

"Looks like this will be an easy crossing but I heard Eli tell the men up front that the next leg will be through some rough country," Jacob reported as he joined the group.

"How's that?" Charles reached for another cake.

"Seems there's a lot of low land, not yet fully dry from the flooding. Could have some trouble with the proverbial Mississippi mud." Jacob leaned over Sarah to get a cup for water. She savored the brush of his arm over her shoulder.

"I've had enough of that gumbo to last a lifetime!" Gray exclaimed.

"Not to mention that red Alabama dirt, never could get the stain out," Cordelia chimed in.

"Eli tells me the soil in Texas will grow anything. According to him it's the land of milk and honey. Can't wait to try him on that boast," Charles repeated Eli's often stated sales pitch.

"Well, we better get the wagons rolling if we're going to get to paradise," Jacob teased as he rose to alert the travelers that rest time had ended and the hard passage was ahead.

Jacob's warning proved up as, after a two-hour crossing through the shallow creek, the teams hit an area of the road practically impassable due to the mud still accumulated and no turnouts to go around. Men, women and children pushed and hollered the beasts through. Some of the lazy boards were given up, to provide traction over the worst patches.

Runwell proved his worth herding the oxen with fierce determination, barking and nipping their heels, moving them forward.

Eli rode up as Jacob bent over to scrape mud from his knee-high boots with a stick. "I think we'll stop up by the next farm. It's abandoned and there's a pond nearby so the folks can clean up a bit."

"We still have several more hours of daylight," Jacob noted. "I am sure the folks will do as you say if you want to press on."

"No, they are exhausted and so am I. I'm not as young as I used to be," Eli chuckled as he rode on along the line to inform the others.

∞∞∞

The wagons began pulling ito the drive to the abandoned farm. After setting up camp the men and women took turns going down to the secluded pond to bathe and wash up mud-caked clothes. The children lingered to swim and frolic. Refreshed from the cooling baths the men scattered and shots rang out as they scoured the nearby woods for game.

Charles and Gray headed for the creek. Jacob took Runwell into the woods to test his mettle as a hunter and found his skills as good as for herding. He mused on the way Sarah snagged scraps for the stray, assuming it was not noticed. He noticed because he could not take his eyes off her. He noticed the way she bit her lip when she concentrated on cooking and sewing—for him, the way she blew escaping curls from her eyes or tucked them behind her ear as she plodded along beside their wagon with no complaint as he fulfilled his dream—not hers, the way those same curls tumbled invitingly down her back at night as she readied for bed in his tent. He could not believe his fortune. He would not deny her anything she desired. He determined the hound was a keeper and knew this would please Sarah.

The women started the fires and took the men's offerings to prepare a blessed meal of fresh rabbit and squirrel. Sarah saw Jacob coming from across the field, a head taller than the rest of the men. His long, steady stride was confident as he called greetings to the others emerging from the trees and whistled for the dog. She thought of her reckless decision to marry and leave her home with this man—a practical stranger—and smiled. Her respect for his leadership grew along with that of the members of the party. Men followed his orders, children hitched rides on his shoulders, older women blushed at his attention, younger women flirted to no avail, even the dog followed at his heels. She was amazed that such a man was hers. But hers to have, and not yet to hold, was proving difficult. She held him only at night when he did not know—when some unknown terror gripped him. She wanted him to heal—to return the embrace.

"How's bout some fiddlin'?" Ben Granger suggested after supper.

"Well, how's bout it?" Eli scanned the area for

his fiddlin' mates, who had packed their instruments as one of their few allotted treasures.

"You're on." One old-timer reached for his instrument.

"Jacob?" Eli prodded.

"I believe I could finger a few tunes." Jacob stood, stretched, then headed to the wagon.

Soon the cacophonous sound of several fiddles tuning at once had everyone's attention. The players struck up the first tune and the crowd forgot the grueling day gone by and concentrated on the amusement at hand. Couples began to pair off in unlikely ways, children to adults, old to young, the conventions of town society thrown off.

Gray and James stood on the edge of the circle with their hands jammed in their pockets. Charles and Carrie whirled with the dancers, appearing lost in the joy of new love.

Jacob watched Sarah as she skipped around the open lawn under the stars and wished to lay down his fiddle and join her. She partnered with Carrie, Mary Jane, Charles, even children anxious to join in the fun. Her cheeks were pink with life and the joy of the dance. He could hear her laughter, rare music to his ears. She glanced at him and smiled each time she passed the porch where he stood to play. Was it an invitation to go to her, to hold her, and be joyful too? The evening ended without a chance to find the answer.

Later, as they readied for bed Sarah carefully worked out of her dress down to her shift, with her back to Jacob, and slipped under the thin sheet on her cot as she usually did. "It was a wonderful evening, thanks for playing."

"My pleasure. I was happy to see you enjoy yourself." Jacob eased his stiff limbs out onto his cot while checking his frustrated thoughts. Then following through on his earlier decision, he gave a low whistle. Runwell peeked his nose inside the tent. "Come on in boy."

Sarah shot him a surprised look.

"Reward for a job well done today. And to keep him safe, for you," he teased.

"Thank you." Runwell lapped at her hands as she settled him down beside her cot. "He reminds me of home, my brothers."

Sarah was not sure she should share her thoughts but took a chance. She was relieved of the sadness that had held her in its grip while she was at home, where memories haunted her. "I felt strangely free tonight, free of the past. But now I feel a bit guilty about that. I don't want to forget my family who are gone."

"Sarah, you cannot grieve forever. I know your brothers would want you to live, to live a happy life for them. I know because I had plenty of time and circumstance to think on how I would want my relations to get on if I did not return. I would never want them to be bound up in grief for me. I chose to fight and if I gave my life, I was happy to do it. I would want them to remember me with happy thoughts."

"I suppose you are right, but I know it will take

time for me to adjust to it. Thank you, for telling me your thoughts."

"I would be grateful if you feel you can come to me anytime, Sarah," Jacob stared at the tent ceiling as he extended his offer.

Jacob fought his phantoms that night and Sarah calmed him once again. He rarely awoke from the night terrors and so did not remember the struggle. The next morning, she broached the subject carefully.

"Last night you said I could come to you with my troubles."

Jacob stopped his packing. "Yes, and I meant it."

"Well, I would like to say the same to you." Sarah fumbled with the clothes she was folding.

"I thank you for the offer." Jacob's gaze lingered on her for a moment then he returned to his packing.

"I mean about your bad dreams," Sarah almost whispered.

Jacob turned to stare. "Have I woken you again?"

"They come more often now. You wake me most every night." Sarah turned to look at him straight on.

"I am sorry. I don't mean to burden you." Jacob reached for her hand, then stopped. His hand dropped to his side.

Sarah reached out and took his clenched hand back. "I want you to tell me your troubles as I will tell you mine."

"Sarah, there are some things a man cannot tell. I cannot speak of what I see in my dreams. It is no fit conversation for a lady." Jacob pulled his hand back and turned to continue his work.

Sarah was at once hurt and mystified that he would offer his solace but not accept hers. She turned back to her folding, her thoughts in turmoil. Perhaps time would draw him out.

"When you are ready to tell me your thoughts, I will be ready to hear them," she offered softly. He finished his packing, lifted the small trunk, and left with no reply.

Chapter 11

Following a well-cut straight line across the state, the wagons rolled through Tupelo and Pontotoc. Then they crossed Mud Creek, among other small tributaries, to Pope's Depot where supplies could be renewed. Turning northwest along the old Chickasaw Nation boundary trail toward Moon Lake, the destination was Trotter's Point, where the ferry would take them across the Mississippi.

"How much to cross?" Charles exclaimed, outraged at the exorbitant figure Jacob quoted.

"One dollar per wagon, 20 cents a head for both large stock and walkers, four cents for sheep, goats and hogs, and fifty cents for men on horseback. Eli says that's 'bout double the last time he crossed, says the ferryman is taking advantage of the large number of refugees coming west." Jacob pulled out his money pouch and began to rifle through the coins to pull the required fees. "Let me know if you need some extra."

"No, I got it this time but if it keeps up at this rate, I'll be on your support by the time we make the Red River."

Charles headed back to his wagon to prepare for the crossing and Jacob followed.

Sarah cinched down bundles to the wagon and pack animals to make sure they would make the trip across the wide river. She was ambivalent as she anticipated setting first foot out of Mississippi into Arkansas. She was sad at leaving her homeland, but eager to finally be on the way into new territory.

"Ready for the ride?" Jacob grinned as he began helping her with the last-minute prep.

"As ready as can be," she gazed out over the river, her shoulders tight with tension.

Jacob came up behind her and placed his hands on her shoulders, massaging the knots that he must have sensed were there, until she began to relax. It was a new sensation to have him touch her in such a comforting way. She closed her eyes and rolled her head from side to side as he worked.

"No need to be afraid. The ferrymen are experts with the loads and stock. It should be an orderly affair." He spoke close to her ear, his breath tickling the stray curls that escaped down her neck.

Her face was so close, her eyes closed, her lips parted in a sigh, it took all his restraint to keep from kissing her for all to see. After all, she was his wife. But he had scrupulously kept his promise to not press her for marital favors. He dropped his hands and her eyes flew open. He eased away from her back. She looked down, smoothed her skirt, and patted her wayward hair into place, as she always did when flustered.

"Sorry, I did not mean discomfit you," Jacob

apologized.

"Oh no, you did not," she met his gaze and gave him a slight smile, "I'm just a bit nervous about leaving my home to venture out into the unknown."

"Well, I'll not lie, so am I. But then I remember that nothing out there can match the fear that a line of charging Yankees can muster," he smiled back, then turned a sobering stare out to the rushing currents of the mighty river.

"I suppose not," her gaze followed his.

"But here I have my family beside me." He reached for her hand. "I have you."

She gave her hand willingly. He pulled it to his lips and kissed it.

They remained in an amiable silence until the ferry-masters sounded the call for them to begin loading.

The crossing took the day to haul 30 wagons, hundreds of stock and people, and other odd attachments across the wide river on two alternating ferries. The men wrangled the wagons and large cattle while the women wrangled the children and small stock. It was exhausting, and at times frightening, as the swift currents caught the ferries and the ferrymen used all their expertise to right the course for a safe landing.

Sarah, Carrie, and Cordelia held their bonnets tightly as they stood at the ferry railings, letting the fine spray splash their faces as they crossed the great Mississippi.

"Can you believe it?" Carrie shouted. "We are bound for the promised land."

"I pray so," Cordelia offered the request for God's blessing.

Sarah held Runwell tight for the ride, his tail thrashing her side from excitement.

When the ferry docked, he jumped from her arms to catch up with Jacob, Charles, and Gray to attend to his herding duties. Sarah laughed with relief that the crossing was finished for the company. Her sadness fell away and a new joy welled up inside. She was headed to her new home with her new family.

∞∞∞

That evening a meeting was called to lay out the course of the next weeks of travel.

"We'll continue northwesterly, avoiding the swampland due west of here, to the Old Military Road and turn back southwest at Little Rock. We'll then continue in a southwest direction staying on the road to the Red River." Eli pointed to the map as he laid out the travel route to the governing group gathered to consider and vote on plans.

"Seems a bit out of the way to keep goin' northerly," a concerned citizen remarked.

"How come we didn't go south to Meridian and take that road west to start with, it all ends up the same place anyhow," another grumbler added his two cents worth.

"Well, gentlemen, if you two had been at the first meetin' you'd have heard the explanation but since you weren't, I'll restate it just for you," Eli answered with frustration. "The southern route is just too burned up and foraged out for us to get supplies. Most of the hard fightin', along with the storm, cleared the country down that way. Trust me, on the northern route, from here on out, the straight-away back country is too hard for man or beast and we need to get to the security of the well-traveled route if we are to be successful. The Indians didn't forge the Southwest Trail for no good reason. The Old Military road follows that route."

The men seemed satisfied with Eli's reasoning and they moved on to other business.

"Anything else on your minds before we quit for tonight?" Jacob moved to wrap things up.

"I have an observation," Deacon Thornton from the Baptist congregation spoke up hesitantly.

"What's on your mind?" Jacob invited him to speak.

"I've heard some talk of gaming in the camp. I thought we ruled against that activity."

"We did. Have you any idea who is involved?" Jacob questioned.

The deacon seemed uncomfortable to be naming names but continued. "Well, that would be Prior Mullens and his party, and some of the younger boys are gettin' involved. If that's so, I thought we might need to nip this in the bud before bad influences get hold of our young ones."

"I see your point. I will look into it," Jacob answered, concealing his personal interest. He had learned the name of the tough who had challenged him over Gray back at the singin' and it was one Prior Mullens. He also noticed that Gray seemed a little pre-occupied of late and in a hurry to break with the group after supper. He determined to keep a closer eye on him. He knew Gray's penchant for flirting with bad company and felt a duty to see if he was involved.

"Well, men, let's break it up, we have a long stretch tomorrow." Eli dispersed the group. He then filled Jacob in on Prior's checkered past as they made their way to their campsites.

"Jacob—be careful. Prior has been a trouble-some sort all during the war. There is nothing too low for him. He deserted at a time he was needed and couldn't be compelled to return to his company. He managed to hide out at his sister's place till the war was over. He has a mean streak and can strike if pro-voked."

"Then how did he become attached to this train? I thought we sifted out outlaws," Jacob bit out.

"He and his gang have been shadowin' us since we left Fulton. I guess you do not know that Mary Jane is his sister. She married Granger at the last minute to come along. You know she's not a bad sort but you can't pick your relatives. She feels responsible for him so she sneaks him food and supplies so he can follow behind us."

"I will keep an eye out for him and see what he is up to." Jacob came to his site and waved Eli off. "Goodnight."

∞∞∞

Jacob undressed and settled onto his cot.

"How did it go tonight?" Sarah was waiting for him as usual. She did not seem to sleep now unless he was with her.

"The same old arguments from the same predictable characters. Had to go over the route again for those who didn't pay attention the last five meetings when we went over it before."

"I am sure you handled the situation admirably."

Jacob could detect her teasing tone but was flattered by her compliment. He turned on his cot to face her. "Sarah, what do you know about Prior Mullens?"

"Mary Jane's brother? He is a scoundrel and a bad influence. Why?" Sarah rolled to face him.

"Some say he has followed us and is causing some trouble, influencing the younger boys to come out and gather at his campsite."

"He lived off Mary Jane during the war after he deserted, hiding out in the countryside, coming in only to get supplies. Everyone knew but none could apprehend him," Sarah recalled the shameful account. "It makes sense he would follow her when she left with us."

"Gray has been leaving the camp in the evenings. I am going to tail him for a while, see what he is up to."

"What makes you think Gray would be involved? I have raised him better than that," Sarah snapped.

Jacob detected her surprise at his insinuation. He chose his words carefully, so he did not implicate Gray further, as he had given Gray his word to keep what he knew from the earlier encounter between the two of them. "I don't suspect him specifically, just thought I might get a drift of what the other boys are saying. If I find Gray is in danger, I will speak to him."

"I would appreciate it if you did not. Tell me and I will handle it."

"Sarah, I do not mean to take over your place in raising Gray, but maybe he needs a man to guide him and I would be glad to help," he offered quietly.

"Just tell me first before you speak if you suspect Gray is in danger," Sarah turned away from him and had the last word.

Jacob was surprised at her rebuke, coming on the heels of her compliment, but resolved to take the business of meddling in her family affairs slowly until she was ready to accept his help.

As the men struck camp at dawn, the women prepared a hearty breakfast that would carry them through the day. Sarah, Cordelia and Carrie worked in tandem to make enough food to serve six people now, and again for a cold lunch on the trail. Sarah turned the conversation from the night before over and over in her head as her hands worked the biscuit dough. She knew Jacob was right. She did not feel adequate for the task of guiding Gray now that he was no longer a child. He did need a man to talk to, but she was not quite ready to relinquish parenting Gray to Jacob. She was still taking Jacob's measure herself.

"Gonna' make Little Rock day after tomorrow." Carrie ventured as she peeled the potatoes and sliced them for panfrying. Runwell devoured the scraps she dropped for him.

"I hear we are going to stop over about a week to give time to rest up and get provisions. I am sure goin' to enjoy seeing a civilized town again," Cordelia answered as she took up the last piece of crispy fried bacon leaving the tasty drippings for the potatoes and griddlecakes to come.

Sarah returned her thoughts to the tasks at hand. She slapped the excess flour from her hands and dumped a pan of fire-roasted coffee beans into the grinder. She gave the lever several turns before pouring the fine grounds into the blue-granite coffee pot and placing it back on the fire to steep.

The men swarmed in, drawn by the strong aromas wafting from the cookfires, and filled up for the grinding march ahead.

"Two more days?" Carrie handed Charles a loaded tin plate.

"Yep, but they will be mighty hard days, I hear. The trail is steep, and the forest is close in, so we must narrow the train to a thin line. "Ladies...be sure and take double care to pack things down tight. It's gonna be rough," Charles offered advice for repacking the wagons.

His prediction was accurate, and the travelers fought to get the jam-packed wagons up and down steep hills and ravines coming into Little Rock. The trail was cut but the road was so narrow and the terrain so rocky that some had to give up their heavier treasures to get the wagons through. As the town came into view the weary pilgrims gave a cheer. Sarah contemplated the few days of rest ahead with relief.

Chapter 12

Jacob came to stand behind Sarah as she fingered the rainbow of ribbons hanging on display in the Little Rock general store. "I heard a rumor 'bout you," his deep voice rumbled softly in her ear, his breath tickled the nape of her neck.

She smiled and answered the challenge, "That being?"

"I heard from a good source that this is a special day and you did not tell me," he continued, standing so close she could smell his clean, familiar scent and feel his warmth at her back.

"I don't tell all my secrets to strange men," she teased.

"Well, being a stranger, I guess it would be improper for me to buy you that ribbon you're eyeing for your birthday?" he countered.

She turned to face him, with a smile to melt butter. "Who told you?"

"Carrie." Jacob seemed to have trouble catching his breath to speak as she was toe to toe with him. Too close for comfort, Sarah imagined. "May I buy you a ribbon, Mrs. McKenna," he whispered the request.

She warmed with the heat of his proximity

and the implication of his words of address, Mrs. McKenna. They had not been intimate in the least but the tone of his address implied possession.

"You may," she accepted.

"Then choose and I will pay," Jacob challenged. She had not yet let him pay for any expense of hers on the trip. She sensed it was important to him to convince her to relinquish the idea that she was still the sole provider for her family. She truly wished to let go of that burden, and the worry of it, that she carried solely on herself. She was beginning to believe that he did not wish to take over, in a dictatorial sense, only to share her burden to lighten it. She had argued with him several times about paying her share. She felt this small offer was well meant so she obliged, picking a lovely rose-colored satin to match the Sunday meeting dress she had stowed away.

"Emeline and Isaac are gonna finally tie the knot," Charles announced the news at supper.

"So's Mattie and Sam." Carrie joined the group with a loaf of fresh baked bread that the Blalocks sent over from the afternoon baking.

Cordelia made her way around the family circle offering more stew before serving herself. "I heard there is quite a bit of excitement since the town's folk heard the circuit preacher is comin'. Last chance for folks to marry before we pull out again."

"The Methodist church agreed to open their doors to the folks wantin' to have a ceremony and all are invited. They sent a rider out to meet the preacher and he has agreed to officiate," Charles continued with the details. "I am sure a good time will be had by all," he grinned at his recent bride. Her face washed a rosy pink.

"Ladies, we will have to exhume our Sunday best from the bottom of the trunks. We can't have weddings in our trail clothes," Cordelia enthused.

Sarah thought of the ribbon Jacob purchased for her. The weddings would be a perfect time to show her appreciation.

Saturday arrived amid a flurry of preparation for the group ceremony that now included three couples from the train. The guests were dressed in their best and crowded into the small church. The organist began to play a processional. Assorted smiling bridesmaids filed down the aisle ahead of the blushing brides. The solemn grooms and their attendants shuffled nervously beside the parson as he fumbled through his bible to locate the appropriate texts.

Jacob's gaze followed his wife down the aisle as she finished the groups entrance behind Carrie and took her place for her part in the ceremony. The rose ribbon he had purchased was laced through her hair, as he longed for his fingers to do. Sarah and Carrie then stepped forward to sing a duet requested by the couples. Sarah glanced around the room then lingered on him briefly before her eyes closed and a sweet hymn floated from her heaven-gifted throat. He closed his eyes to let her voice flow over and into him. Soon she squeezed into the over-crowded pew beside him, meshed into his side as Eve to Adam. The preacher's words of union between a man and his wife taunted him.

Sarah felt Jacob tense as she wedged into his side. His warmth was contagious, and she had to fan herself continuously as the vows evoked the ideal of the union between a man and woman that God ordains. The tension between them was intense and unsettling. She was not sure she understood the cause. Was Jacob angry? Was he resentful of their arrangement? She could only decipher her own tension—it was a growing need. She needed him, his touch, his attention, his love.

The festivities lasted well into the night. Jacob stalked her, catching a few dances. Sarah felt each partnering incited him more than the last. He pulled her as close as decency allowed in public, even between the married folks. She felt the intensity in his touch, and it was contagious. She knew a fire was kindled. Would it grow into the blaze she felt was inevitable?

As the party broke up, they walked in silence to the campsite.

"I am going for a walk," Jacob dismissed her suddenly and veered off the path just ahead of the clearing, leaving her to go on alone.

Cordelia caught up from behind them to finish the distance. "I almost hate to move on. We've made so many new acquaintances here."

"True." Sarah slowed down to meet her mother-in-law's gait.

"But our new home is bound to hold some surprises not to be missed," Cordelia made conversation sensing Sarah's mood. "You alright?"

Sarah was startled, from her pensive reflection on the path under her feet, by the probing question. "Of course."

"You just seem a little down to me. Everything okay between you and Jacob?" Cordelia continued like a physician with a needle to an angry boil—only way it can heal is to excise it.

"Everything is fine." Sarah forged ahead on the path, avoiding the examination.

"I am sorry. I do not mean to pry. I just sense you two are having a hard time what with the lack of privacy and the demands of the trip and all. Not much of a honeymoon I'd guess." Cordelia caught up and reached for Sarah's hands.

"Sometimes I feel Jacob is angry with me and I cannot see a reason why," Sarah confided.

"When a man needs his wife the most, he often pushes her away the hardest. No rhyme or reason to it, just the way they are. Just be patient. He will come to you when the time is right." Cordelia squeezed Sarah's hands as she spoke.

Sarah broke the contact, embarrassed. Had Cordelia rightly discerned the struggle she was having with the unusual confines of the train and its hindrance on their ability to grow closer naturally to the God ordained conclusion? She was shocked by her own bold thoughts but knew that she now wanted to belong to Jacob—soul—and body.

Jacob ploughed through the brush and into the woods. His head pounded with the self-imposed admonition that he must check his growing passion for his wife. He felt frustrated by the confines of train life, the constant scrutiny of their trail mates. At times he thought he felt a bond growing between himself and his bride. He wanted to pursue it to the logical conclusion but was wary of pushing too hard, afraid to learn his advances might be unwelcome. He stopped thrashing through the forest and pounded his fist into the nearest tree. He shook the pain off his hand and slid down to sit at the base of the pine to cool off.

As his breathing slowed, he tried to redirect his thoughts from how Sarah filled his arms at the wedding dance just an hour before. Voices up ahead on the footpath broke his concentration.

"Come on Gray, keep up. You gonna get eat up

by a critter if you don't stay with us."

"Shut up, James. There's no big animal signs around here, too close to town," Gray panted, short of breath. "You sure you know where you're goin'?"

"Yeah, I been out here the other night."

On alert, once he heard Gray's voice, Jacob quietly rose and began to tail the pair as they made their way along the path, following another group ahead. They soon came to a clearing where a lively game of dice was in progress.

Jacob stationed himself where he could see, but not be seen. He determined to let the evening play out as he gathered information for confrontation later. Prior Mullens, the ringleader as suspected, strutted like a peacock between the participants. He urged them to up the ante. Most were losing precious dollars they could not afford to part with as it would be months before they were settled and able to replace them.

By morning most of the victims had staggered back to town. Jacob stepped out in Gray's path as he headed toward their campsite. "I believe we had an agreement about this sort of entertainment."

Gray looked up, startled, as Jacob came out of the woods to his right and into the path. "I didn't make you any promises," he snarled.

"Well, I made you one. I would tell Sarah about your new associates and activities if you kept it up. Can you give me good reason not to?" Jacob kept pace as Gray sped up to get ahead of his accuser.

"Go ahead, she can't stop me, and neither can

you."

Jacob stepped in front of Gray, blocking his way. "You know Gray, the Bible says there is a way that seems right to a man, but the way thereof is death. You are playing with fire and getting burned is just the first thing that can happen. Men like Prior Mullens court death and drag along all who follow them. I don't want Sarah to have to bury her last brother."

Gray pushed past his tormentor. "Don't go quotin' the Book to me, like her. Just 'cause you married my sister doesn't make you my brother. You got no claim on me. You mind your business and I'll mind mine."

∞∞∞

When Jacob did not return, Sarah became concerned. It was late. He had headed off onto the forest path. Dangers lurked in the dark. She knew it was irrational to worry about a grown man, but he was her man...her life. She could not sleep without him there. She picked up his old chambray shirt, settled cross-legged onto her cot, and squinted in the candlelight to continue the mend she was making before washing it. The well-worn fabric was soft and fragile. She held it up to breathe in his unique scent that enticed her when he was near. Tears of frustration filled the corners of her eyes. The night air was cooling, and she shuddered with the slight chill. She slipped her arms into the sleeves and wrapped the comforting garment around her slight frame. As she lay down wrapped in his essence, sleep captured her against her will.

Jacob let Gray go, knowing he would have to confront him again and hoped he would be able to make him see reason eventually. He made his way wearily back to camp. As he lifted the tent flap, he saw his love. Yes, he had to admit it, he loved her so that he ached. The sight of her sleeping flowed into his mind and with it the delighted surprise that she was curled up in his old blue chambray shirt, the one he wore when he first laid eyes on her.

Chapter 13

In early October nature began a color show along the route toward the Red River, splashing the forests along the trail with brilliant yellow, gold, orange and red, with a swath of purple dabbed in for playful contrast. Even the sky was a brighter blue, the light more intense. The weather was perfectly cool for traveling and the company was in high spirits.

The travelers chattered each evening around the fires describing plans for lush farms, cattle, horse and sheep ranches, and building new lives in a time of peace.

Jacob imagined it was the same for the children of Israel in the desert headed for the land of milk and honey. He had concerns about the high expectations and naive exaggeration about the ease with which they would conquer the land.

"I hear there is a bit of a dust up between the sheep ranchers and the cattlemen," Charles rumored as he inspected his repair to the tack he was working on.

"Seems to be more a central Texas fight. We'll be further north and out of their way," Jacob assured as he tended to a broken harness.

"We still goin' to head out to the Nolan River, out past Fort Worth?"

"Seems the best course to me. Eli and several others are goin' out that far and he says his sister assures him the Indians are mostly peaceable and the land is good and plentiful," Jacob confirmed as he rose from the short camp stool and stretched his stiff legs.

"Eli's word is good enough for me." Charles began to clear the campsite for an early start the next morning. "Night, brother."

Jacob offered the scraps from his plate to Runwell with an amused grin. Carrie was the usual tender heart, but this pitiful cur had won the affection of his beloved Sarah. The hound proved his worth as a hunter and herder, so he was beginning to care for him too.

He found Sarah sitting cross-legged on her cot going through a small bag of her most prized treasures, as if to catalog them once again. He had memorized them by now: a handkerchief full of peach pits to seed the new orchard she intended to plant, her mother's amethyst brooch, packets of flower seeds she had purchased in Little Rock, a bundle of letters from William tied with string sitting on top of the family Bible, neatly rolled ribbons including the one he bought for her. This occasional accounting of her special things amused him. He sat down on his cot and pulled off his heavy boots.

"What in the world is that?" he laughed at his bride as she carefully unwrapped a clod of dirt and peered at it as if it was a precious stone.

"Mississippi mud." She held it out for him to inspect. "Reminds me of home."

"I'd have thought you'd be glad to be rid of it." He grinned sideways at her.

"I thought so too until the other day, when I saw the dirt clods that had been hanging onto the wagon let go, one by one. I realized soon they would all be gone and with them the soil I was born on would be behind me. I had to save just a small bit. It's silly, I know, but it comforts me to have it." She carefully rewrapped the dried earth and put it away with the rest of her mementos and blew out the lantern.

Jacob mused, as he drifted off to sleep, that Sarah had dreams too: a new home with flowers around the porch, a peach orchard to give the golden fruit for her delicious preserves, maybe dresses to match her ribbons and her mother's brooch, continued faith and fond memories of her old home and family. He prayed to help deliver these gifts.

Sarah woke with a start at Jacob's shout. The night terrors were more frequent and intense now. She often wrestled Jacob to keep the camp from rousing at his frantic shouting of orders and cursing the enemy. She knew he was on some distant battlefield that she could not reach to calm him. He clawed the air urgently speaking in quick, demanding gibberish that then became intelligible.

"Charles, Charles!" Jacob was shouting and trying to push an invisible load from above him. He thrashed violently as Sarah tried to subdue him.

"Get off me, you cursed blue-belly." He swung wildly knocking Sarah to the floor. He swiped at his face and held his hand up before his eyes as if inspecting it.

The blood dripped from his hand. Was it his own or that from the bodies atop him? He struggled to push the heavy weight from above him. He was buried under several layers of lifeless human flesh. Buried alive. The stench of the battlefield engulfed him. The slick red ooze, covering everything in his trapped position, had long grown cold. He gave another mighty heave and the bodies rolled to the side and freed him from his premature grave. He struggled to stand and surveyed the grisly scene, stretched out the length of the rocky slope, where the recent battle was tried. A sea of blue and gray splashed with great swaths of red met his still blurred vision. As his head cleared, the true horror of the battlefield zoomed into focus: Yankees and Rebels still locked in death grips where they fell, limbs scattered from the rain of cannon fire over the hillside. Blood. Blood everywhere. Rivers of blood. Then his thoughts raced to his brother. Charles. Where is Charles? He began to climb over the bodies, to frantically search every gray-uniformed man, looking into the ashen faces of childhood friends and newly met company mates, to call out as he went, "Charles, Charlie!"

"Charles, Charlie!" Jacob struggled against Sarah.

"It's alright, Jacob. Charles is alright. He is here with us. The war is over," she crooned.

Jacob relaxed into her arms and his large frame shuddered as he began to sob, "Charlie, where are you? I'm sorry, I'm sorry. I told Mama I would keep you safe, where are you?"

Sarah began to hum the melody of the lullaby she often sang to calm him and then added the words, *"Hush little baby, don't say a word, Mama's gonna' buy you a mockingbird. . ."*

Unlike times before, Jacob began to rouse from his fitful sleep. Sarah tried to disengage from the lock she had on him, but he came awake as she was un-wrapping her legs from around his long frame, her nightgown ruched up to her knees and her arm caught under his head.

"What the devil?" Jacob, half awake, tried to scooch away from the foreign body in is bed.

Sarah could not make her escape from his territory this time, so she made a quick decision that this was the time to confront him about these episodes. "Jacob, wake up. You were having that bad dream again, I had to quiet you, or you would wake the whole camp."

Jacob tried to sit up but entangled as he was, he could not. He fell back into her. Fully awake, he took in the length of shapely leg running along-side his own and his whole body clenched. He felt the moisture on his face and reached up to swipe the remnants of tears from his stubbled cheek. "I've been blubbering like a baby, haven't I?" he sighed.

"Yes, but you should not be ashamed. You have been through such trials you need a release, Jacob. Maybe if you tell me what you see in those dreams you can let it go." It took all her strength to will her hands to her sides, to not stroke his arms, his face, to soothe the tension she felt in him. "I asked you to share your troubles with me and I am strong enough to hear what you need to say."

After a tentative silence he relaxed against her and relented. "It was so terrible—the war. So many men died, and for what?" His bitterness surged up and came flowing out. "The battles around Chattanooga haunt me the most. Both sides gave it all they had. We had been camped on the side of the mountain for weeks in the cold and rain. The men were sent down to hospital in droves, the conditions were so bad. Then we were forced into battle along the ridges of Lookout Mountain, close fighting, hand to hand. The men fought and died, in each other's arms. The bodies were piled three-deep in some places. I was buried under the layers. I had to push my way out."

Tears flowed down his face as he recounted his search for Charles only to find that he had been sent down to hospital and his condition was unknown. He later learned that Charles suffered a severe leg wound.

"I promised Mama I would keep him safe. A lot of men died in that campaign. Most of the company from home was wiped out. I don't know why I am the one who lived." His breathing slowed. His story was finished.

Sarah was quiet for a time, then offered the only answer she had. "You lived for me." Jacob did not hear her. He had drifted back to sleep, a peaceful sleep, at last.

∞∞∞

"Won't be as hard a crossing as the Mississipp'; but secure the load as tight as can be." Jacob fished in his vest pocket for the tiny slit into the inner lining where he had secured several gold coins and various change. He drew out enough to cover the ferryman's fees to cross the Red River to the Texas side.

"Texas at last." Sarah prepared to leave Arkansas and set first foot on their new homeland.

"Yes, my dear bride, a Texican at last," Jacob grinned, speaking the endearment he often used now when addressing her.

My dear bride. Sarah reveled in the warmth of his playful address. It seemed a barrier had come down after he confided his dream to her. He had since shared more painful memories allowing his spirit to begin healing. She felt the sharing was weaving their souls into a new tapestry, one tapestry.

"I hear the village at the landing is well set up for wintering over with so many passing through. I still just hate the idea of stopping for three months," Sarah sighed.

"Eli said the rains start in November and sometimes turn to ice or snow in December and January. He says the trail will be impassable until early spring. I keep telling myself at least it's not forty years to get to our promised land," Jacob teased and pecked her on the cheek before moving to the landing to pay their fees.

Sarah savored his spontaneous gestures. They were becoming more common.

When Jacob returned it was time to load. Sarah, Cordelia, and Carrie followed behind the wagon as the men "gee" and "hawed" the skittish oxen onto the ferry. The float across the red-stained water was short but the effect on the party was evident in the whistles, shouts, and celebrating that erupted as each group disembarked onto Texas soil.

Charles awkwardly danced Carrie around the red dirt bank singing 'The Yellow Rose of Texas' at the top of his lungs.

"I thought that song was about a woman of dubious repute, sir!" Carrie shouted over him merrily.

"But she was a heroine of the republic too," Charles stole a kiss before Carrie could dodge him. They fell onto the blanket Cordelia had laid out for lunch. He rose again and tugged at her to join him.

"Charles, no more, I cannot," she looked at him intently, sending a silent message. He returned her gaze in agreement.

Cordelia caught the exchange, "Is there something you two would like to share with us?" she teased.

Charles noted the nod from Carrie and announced as she blushed, "We are increasing the population of Texas, not by two but three,"

"Well, I'll be jiggered!" Gray burst out. "I'm gonna' be an uncle!"

"Congratulations, you two." Jacob reached over to pump Charles' hand.

"Praise God I'll be a Grandmother." Cordelia beamed, squeezing Carrie's hand. "I thought I might not live to see the day. Carrie, I thought I detected a special glow lately. How long have you known?"

"Two months." Carrie blushed again.

"Mighty fast work, brother." Jacob knocked Charles in the shoulder.

"Couldn't help myself with such a beautiful bride," Charles shot back as Carrie tried to shush him.

With all the ballyhoo around her during the meal, Sarah sat quietly soaking in the announcement and its implications. Charles' and Carrie's love had bloomed into a new life that would be the first of their McKenna clan to be born on Texas soil. She was filled with joy for them and a bit of envy as well. She wondered if her love for Jacob would ever draw him to her in the same way. Would she ever glow with the knowledge that she carried his gift of life as Carrie carried Charles'? The news also brought fear for her younger sister. Having a child back home in the best of circumstances was fraught with peril but out on the prairie it was downright dangerous.

"Sarah, are you angry with me?" Carrie nudged Sarah out of her heavy thoughts.

"Of course not, Carrie." Sarah smiled and stroked her sister's cheek. "I am overjoyed to hear your news."

"I wanted to tell you sooner but did not want you to worry. I am fit as a fiddle. I have had no sickness. I am not tired. I feel exhilarated," Carrie reassured her excitedly.

"Then I am more than pleased."

"Ladies, time to pack up if we want to see our winter home before dark." Jacob shooed them from the blanket. He shared the task of folding it with Sarah, his fingers touching hers as they "kissed" the corners. Her gaze locked with his for a moment, then they continued the domestic routine to its completion. Charles' and Carrie's news deeply affected her, crystallizing her growing need for him. Sarah determined that moment, when she sensed a question in his expression, it was time to let Jacob know her feelings for him had changed. She needed him like she needed air, water, food. He had become a necessity for her life. She loved him.

As the tingle in his hands subsided, Jacob watched his wife as she gracefully moved about the picnic site to repack their things to move on. His reaction to Charles' news was to bring his own dilemma into focus. Jacob felt the intense force of his need for Sarah drawing him toward a reckoning. He knew he could not continue the pretense of indifference when his body and soul hungered so intensely for her. He loved her. He would have to lay his feelings bare to her and face the consequences.

Chapter 14

Scouts returned with a report of the conditions at a nearby lake. The village folks suggested it as a campsite. Many previous pioneers found it a satisfactory stopping point during the long months of North Texas winter. The water was good, the game plentiful and the trail was well-cut and easy to accommodate trips to town when supplies were needed. The enclosing forest would provide some protection from the anticipated wind and rain. Small shelters might also be built from the abundant timber.

Jacob and Charles were more than eager to choose sites for an extended stopover, and they set about making their temporary home as snug and comfortable as the meager supplies could afford. They began building a crude one room cabin that would be shelter for the coldest months. They also constructed half-faced shelters over the tents to make them more weather-proof for milder days. Gray and James Blalock requested permission to construct their own quarters mid-way between the family sites, learning much needed skills for pioneer life. The congregation of refugees, from other trains also stopping to take advantage of the natural amenities surrounding the lake, grew into a sizable camp as the fall days short-ened toward winter.

"What you got there, brother?" Charles nodded toward the stack of prime walnut logs that Jacob was concealing in the underbrush.

"Well, it's none of your business, and you scared the wits out of me sneaking up that way. Christmas is coming and I have determined to make Sarah some-thing special. I'm only telling you because I may need your help to get this load to the sawmill in town. I can't trust you to keep your mouth shut if you think I am lurking about in the forest hiding perfectly good wood from the others." Jacob propped his hands on his hips and glared at his brother, daring him to keep the secret.

"Secret's safe with me. What you thinking about building?" Charles began helping to arrange the logs in the thick underbrush.

"Sarah's not got enough storage for her special things so I thought a trunk might be welcomed."

"You know your reputation with a nail and hammer." Charles nodded toward Jacob's hand. "Would you like some help?"

"You just can't let that smashed thumb I got when I was twelve go can you little brother."

"You were my hero, I thought you could do any-thing till I saw that mangled thumb you got building me a fort down by the creek."

"Yeah, I've disappointed you ever since," Jacob replied soberly.

Charles straightened to address his brother directly, "No, I have never been disappointed, and you need to stop dwelling on the past. You have always been there for me. I wouldn't be standing here if that wasn't the truth." Charles indicated his leg as he continued, "You carried me straight out of that field hospital and saved my leg when old Saw-bones was about to do his best to make me a permanent cripple. Then you nursed me for days as the fever took me. I'll be forever grateful to you."

Jacob ran his hand through his hair nervously as he shrank before such praise. "I just feel I could have done better for you and Mother."

"Nonsense, only God could have seen us through the war unscathed and that would have been unfair to all the others who were hurt. We bring these things on ourselves and we have to take our lickin' for our foolishness."

"You thinking of taking up preaching, that sounds like a good sermon," Jacob teased.

"Just trying to talk some sense into you so you will stop trying to carry the world around on your own shoulders."

"That's what Sarah says too."

"A wise woman, told you she would do you good."

"And I am forever grateful to you for that. She is all things good for me." Jacob turned to continue his chore, unable to share any more of his private thoughts, and the two worked in silence until the light was gone.

∞ ∞ ∞

"One, two, three...," Jacob and Charles hoisted the third whole log onto the borrowed buckboard and headed to town. The sawmill planed the raw wood into usable boards of various sizes for building.

Jacob counted out the fee and motioned Charles toward the general store.

Each had his own list from their ladies. Once threads and notions were located and staples were replenished, then they could inspect the hardware and tools.

Jacob held up a sharp implement for Charles' inspection. "How about his carving tool? I remember how you loved to carve when we were kids. Thought I might get you to put some initials on Sarah's box."

"I can just use my pocketknife. That's expensive." Charles turned the special tool over and over in his hand.

"Just call it an early Christmas gift if you'll do some carving for me," Jacob cajoled.

"It's your money, so deal." Charles accepted.

Back at the work site the wood was unloaded, and Jacob began to separate it into two stacks.

"What are you doing?" Charles interrupted.

"This stack is for me." Jacob indicated one with larger sizes. Waving his hand over a stack with smaller pieces he continued. "This is for you."

"What for?" Charles laughed.

"Payment for doing some carving and my gift for a cradle for my new nephew. Or were you going to have him sleep in a hammock swinging from the trees?" Jacob retorted.

"Well that is generous recompence for a bit of doodling, and how do you know my *daughter* won't like swinging from a tree?"

"Well, just to be on the safe side, make the cradle and carve one of your fancy doodles on it as well." Jacob slapped the tool into Charles hand with a grin.

"And when can I expect to see a niece or nephew from you and Sarah? My youngin' will need some company out on the range."

Jacob pretended to not hear the question.

"What was that brother? I didn't hear you," Charles teased as the silence continued.

Jacob banged a nail with unnecessary force.

"Oh...I see. You haven't touched her, have you?" Charles sobered.

"No, and I'll thank you to keep it to yourself. She has made no indication she is agreeable to it."

Charles slapped his forehead and turned a circle. "Good Lord, man! You don't see the way she looks at you? Her eyes follow you everywhere you go. It's plain to everyone but you!"

"We never spoke of that kind of marriage." Jacob kept working, head down.

Charles raked his hand through his hair, "Well, what other kind is there...oh...no, no, no. You can't be serious!"

"I am. I won't force her." Jacob pitched his chisel

in frustration.

"Of course. Well then, get busy talking. You act like a love-sick buck. Just go in and tell her how you feel."

"You don't know Sarah. She's got a mind of her own and I respect that. We never talked about it. It is sort of understood."

"Well, I believe you will be surprised if you talk to her. Tell her your feelings have changed and maybe hers have too. Will you think about it? No sense in you two being miserable."

"If you leave me be, I will." Jacob retrieved his tool and returned to work.

For the next several weeks they worked together to finish the winter cabin and to surreptitiously fashion their gifts before the holiday. Jacob felt at peace when working with the wood to remove the rough edges, to smooth the uneven places. He thought of Sarah as he worked; the many small things she did for him each day. He thought of her seated near the campfire, the light dancing on her golden hair as she mended his shirts and socks, sewed on his buttons. He imagined her bent over the wash, the cook-fire. He was grateful for the stoop labor she performed for her family's comfort, for his comfort. He wanted the chest to be perfect, a perfect offering symbolizing his love for her. He wanted her to understand that the chest for her special things was meant to convey that what was important to her was also important to him.

∞∞∞

The women also made plans. As the month of November ended the excitement began to build for the weeks of preparation for a celebration of Christ's birth in the wilderness. Small gifts were made in secret. With several new trains arriving around the lake, the talk centered on shared holiday traditions and new ones never heard before.

"A tree...in the house?" Cordelia exclaimed as she punched the bread dough and folded it over for another whack.

"Ja...we choose a small evergreen and bring it in for decorating. We use berries, paper cuttings, cookies and candles are lit on the branches on Christmas Eve." Helga Wagner, a German emigrant whose train was bound for Fredericksburg, explained as she placed dough into a pan and shoved it to the middle of the long plank table under the trees where the ladies were preparing the days bread for baking.

"I never heard the like." Mattie Blalock placed a pan of dough onto a long paddle and shoved it into the oven.

"It is very festive; you must try it. There are plenty of such small trees here. I will show you when we prepare ours."

"I would love to see it," Carrie chimed in as she dusted her flour covered hands onto her apron. "Sarah, what are you planning for Jacob?"

"I haven't thought of anything yet, I want it to be special." Sarah pushed a wisp of unruly curl from her eyes, smudging her nose white in the process.

The men invaded their space at that moment. Charles pinched a piece of raw dough as Carrie slapped his hand. He reciprocated with a peck on her neck.

Sarah sensed Jacob close behind her and she turned to face him. He reached for the errant curl and tenderly tucked it behind her ear, smiling that enigmatic smile he had adopted lately. She felt she could discern its meaning. He wanted her as she wanted him. But she could not be sure, so she kept herself tightly in check when around him. Then he softly rubbed the smudge from her nose as he stared directly into her eyes. Her breath caught as she measured the longing she detected there. She determined then what his gift would be.

∞∞∞

"Carrie, I need to speak with you." Sarah caught her sister returning from the lake with water and took the pails from her as they continued to the campsite.

Carrie stopped at a fallen log beside the path, "Sit and we will talk. Now what is it you need?"

"How did you know when Charles wanted more from you than friendship?" Sarah did not know how to phrase the questions she needed to ask.

Carrie needed no coaching, she addressed Sarah's unspoken request. "I am sure you know. I could see it in his eyes, his attentions to me. And judging by the looks you two have been sharing, I am sure Jacob feels the same for you."

"Oh, is it that apparent?" Sarah was embarrassed. "I think I am feeling his attachment growing but I am not sure. Do you believe so too?"

"I am sure of it. I know love-struck looks when I see them"

Carrie took Sarah's hands in her own. "I guess your situation is a bit different than mine. I know you and Jacob made an agreement to marry to keep the families together. But we all can see that you two truly care for one another and are frustrated by your own stubborn refusal to let go of the rules you imposed in that agreement."

"How can I let him know I am ready without being too bold? You know he has not touched me as a wife."

"Now Sarah, you cannot be too bold in telling the man you love how you feel. He may be more afraid of making a declaration than you are, so the thing to do is just tell him. Don't be embarrassed to show the love that God has given you, it is a great gift."

Sarah fidgeted at Carrie's amused tone. "I cannot think Jacob is afraid of me."

"Well, just as you are afraid of offending him, he may be also afraid to speak his heart to you."

"I will think about it. Thank you for hearing me out."

"It is my pleasure to help you if I can with anything that troubles you. You are my dear sister. I can only wish you the great joy in your love that I have found in mine."

Chapter 15

The weather grew colder as the mood of the temporary campers grew warmer with anticipation of the coming holiday. Furtive activity surrounding secrets being kept, and open preparation for a proper ceremony to mark the sacred date, was well underway. The Mississippi travelers were in negotiations with the German settlers to share traditions from each group to make all feel as merry as the makeshift campsite would allow.

"Ja, glass ornaments made in the shape of fruits, toys, and angels are hung on the tree. Then we bake cookies to add for the children," Helga explained the German traditions of decorating a tree as the group of ladies worked on the American addition of berry garlands for the cedar that had been erected in the center of the campsite for decorating.

"Here are some more berries," a gaggle of willing children shouted as they returned, cheeks pinked, from the walk to the woods to hunt for the red berries the ladies were stringing with Helga's helpful guidance.

"Soon we will bake the cookies," Helga reminded the group.

"Cookies!" The children shouted with glee as they ran around and through the group.

"Go back out and find some of those pinecones for us." She shooed them on to another manufactured task.

"So, you have the forms for the cookies and the recipe for the dough from your country?" Cordelia held up her string, now several feet long.

"I do and it is simple. They should bake well enough in our bread ovens. If we all come out, we will get the job done in no time."

"Are you going to hide the pickle, Oma?" Helga's youngest grandson asked expectantly.

"I will if you wish."

"A pickle?" Carrie laughed as the tow-headed boy nodded his ascent.

"Yes. It is a good story, this idea of placing a pickle in the tree branches." Helga grinned in anticipation of sharing another story.

"Tell us," Carrie urged her to share.

"A Bavarian man from our home in Pennsylvania went to fight on the Union side. He was captured and spent months in the prison at Andersonville. He was starving. He saw a guard eating pickles one day and begged for just one. The guard took pity and gave him one. He told us that as he ate the juicy treat slowly as he could, he savored the spicy taste, the knobby texture. He vowed, if he lived, to never forget that small kindness and the joy of eating that simple pickle. The first Christmas, after he returned home by God's grace, he placed a small pickle deep inside the branches in his tree to remind him of the miracle that he was alive. The small act of the Rebel guard, the gift of the pickle, had renewed his will to live. When his eldest child noticed a pickle in the tree branches on Christmas morning the man related the story, and its lesson, rewarding the child's keen eye with the choice of the first cookie from the tree."

"Can we do it, Oma, can we?" The children echoed Helga's grandson in the chant.

"As I have brought along a few jars, we will do it. You must go to bed early to have the clearest eyes to find it."

The children skipped away, chattering.

∞∞∞

The days were counted down to Christmas as Sarah contemplated just how to approach Jacob. She did not want to begin a new year as they were, separated by an understanding that no longer made sense. The New Year called for a new resolution. She wanted to tell Jacob of her feelings for him. She wanted to celebrate their love.

Carrie caught up with her as she came back from gathering kindling for the campfire.

"The cabin is almost finished. It should be ready by Christmas. I cannot wait for a night with a real roof over my head. Charles and I are gonna lock ourselves in for a week." Carrie matched her gait as they ambled up the path.

Sarah laughed at her sister's declaration. "That long? What about the rest of us? It may get mighty cold out here come January."

"Well, I guess that would be a bit selfish. We will give it up for you and Jacob to have a little privacy. How about New Year's Eve?" Carrie teased.

"That's alright, you two go ahead and enjoy it. We will all be forced inside together soon enough." Sarah tried to deflect Carrie's offer.

Carrie stopped in the middle of the trail and faced her sister. "You have not spoken to Jacob, have you?" she accused with a smile.

"No." Sarah did not deny her reluctance to confront Jacob.

"What will I do with you two lovebirds," Carrie teased.

"I have not found the right time," Sarah defended herself.

"Any time is the right time, silly goose. Promise me you will do it soon," Carrie demanded.

"I will, I will," Sarah agreed, not sure she could work up her courage to make the first move no matter how much she wanted to be with her husband in more than name only.

That evening Carrie and Charles sat huddled away from the group at supper. Sarah was not comfortable with the glances the two threw her way. They seemed to be discussing her. Her thoughts were racing as she worried the idea of approaching Jacob. He sat nearby, disturbing her senses. She could see no way past her shyness in expressing her inner-most thoughts. She was not one to blurt her feelings on any subject, let alone those concerning her growing need for her husband. She ate silently.

"You feeling alright?" Jacob questioned as they readied to bed down for the night.

"I'm fine," Sarah lied.

"Seem awfully quite tonight."

"Just tired." Sarah climbed onto her cot and pulled up the warm cover. Jacob blew out the lamp and she could hear the creak of the cot accepting his weight. Maybe the cover of dark would give her confidence to speak. As she heard him shift to find a comfortable position on the hard bed, she knew tonight would not be the time. She turned to the tent wall and tears of frustration pooled in her closed eyes.

∞ ∞ ∞

"Thanks for your help with the trunk. I did not want to have Sarah see it till Christmas. I think taking it to the cabin is the best idea." Jacob stacked wood scraps into a small pile as he and Charles cleaned their work site in the woods.

"My pleasure, and same with the cradle. The ladies will surely be surprised."

"I know Carrie will be happy to have a night in warmth and comfort when we get the cabin finished." Jacob grinned conspiratorially at Charles.

"Yeah, I am looking forward to next week," Charles mused.

"I reckon you are," Jacob teased. "Well, I am happy for you both."

"Well, you and Sarah can have it to yourselves the next week, wouldn't want to be selfish," Charles offered.

Jacob noticed the bubbling mirth just under the surface of Charles' smile.

"No, Carrie needs the shelter, you know, in her condition," Jacob hurried to decline the offer.

"Don't be so chivalrous brother. My bride is hardy and yours could use some pampering too." Charles headed down the path to the campsite as if the matter was settled.

Jacob followed, deep in thoughts of Sarah and privacy and all the love he wanted to share with her. He just did not know how to approach her. They had an agreement and he could not think of how to ask her to amend it. He might lose the little companionship they already shared. He would not risk that. With God's help, he would keep tight rein on his personal desires.

∞ ∞ ∞

On Christmas Eve the ladies and children worked together to hang the garland and cookies on the communal tree, in preparation for the service to be held that night. They practiced all the carols they collectively knew.

As the stars began to blink in the clear black

sky, the pilgrims streamed to the clearing from all directions, circling the gaily decorated fir tree as planned. The mood was quiet and reverent. In the tradition of the singin's back home they took a key, finding the note from Eli, and vocalized the first carol, *God Rest You Merry Gentlemen*. Sarah could feel the warmth of Jacob's body as he stood just behind her. The timbre of his baritone voice mingled with her soprano. Vocally, they were a perfect match. They moved on to newer tunes, *Oh, come all ye faithful, Hark the herald angels sing*. The third verse of *It came upon a midnight clear* expressed the anguish and then hope for recovery that the war worn travelers experienced,

> "Yet with the woes of sin and strife
> The world has suffered long
> Beneath the angel strain have rolled
> Two thousand years of wrong
> And man, at war with man, hears not
> The love song which they bring
> O hush the noise ye men of strife
> And hear the angels sing!"

Harmonizing with Jacob was effortless, joyful. Sarah warmed thinking of the gift she wanted to give to her love. Would they harmonize effortlessly in this new intimacy, joyfully, as when they worked side by side or sang the tunes handed down for generations? Would they begin a new generation to carry the family on?

After singing several more carols, Eli read the

Christmas Story. Then Jacob stepped out as planned, placed his fiddle to his chin, and closed his eyes to gather strains that the universe hummed on this Holy Night. He drew out his soul onto the strings in the newly learned German tune, *Silent Night*. The pilgrims worshiped silently as the fiddle-master wove the prayerful tune among them to conclude the evening. The crowd dispersed quietly to their campsites where personal celebrations would continue.

"What have you there?" Jacob asked as he entered the tent after checking the campsite for the night.

In the dim kerosene lamp light, Sarah bent over her sewing in concentration.

"I am finishing a "journey quilt" for the baby. I have made scenes from our journey on squares and now I am checking them for any stray threads. I thought our little McKenna would need to know the story of how we became Texans." Sarah held the almost finished quilt top up for his inspection.

"Ah, a novel idea. Carrie will love it." Jacob leaned in to inspect the delicate thread work.

Sarah was overwhelmed by his proximity. She fumbled to pull back without giving offense.

Jacob backed up and turned to the tent opening. "I have something for you."

He returned with a large wooden chest, bending under its weight to get it inside the tight space.

"Come," he instructed as he set it down at the foot of her cot.

Sarah scrambled to comply and stood beside him as he opened the lid.

"It is a chest for your special things." Jacob looked into her eyes.

He had taken note of her special things, the things that mattered to her. He unlocked his gaze to close the lid and she saw the beautiful carving in the center of the top.

It was her initials with the M for McKenna in the center. She ran her fingers over the grooves. It was as if he had carved his brand onto her heart. She backed away, longing to speak the words she had rehearsed so many times in the past few days. I love you. I need you. I want you.

Instead she quickly turned and retrieved a cloth bundle from under her cot. "This is for you."

Jacob took the bundle and slowly opened it. He looked at the strange bag pieced together from soft skins with a leather cord drawstring. "It is a bag to protect your fiddle. I am told that water will not penetrate the specially prepared hide."

Sarah waited for his reaction as he inspected it. He was standing so close she could feel his body move as he breathed. Then he looked into her eyes again. A small grin playing at the corners of his beautiful lips was the only sign that her gift was pleasing. His gaze moved to her mouth as he spoke.

"May I, Mrs. McKenna?"

Sarah knew his intent by instinct. She breathlessly nodded her assent.

His lips feathered hers, as a sweet introduction, then he pressed more urgently as he laid his free hand on her waist. Then as she tip-toed up to meet him he broke the embrace, leaving her tossing on a sea of sensations.

Jacob turned and left the tent. Sarah was frustrated and hurt. She knew she could not continue this way.

Jacob walked off his frustration under the crystal-clear canopy of stars. He knew the limits of his restraint were about to snap. He loved, needed, wanted his wife. He left her because he knew that it was not the time or place to declare his intentions to renegotiate their arrangement, when they did not even have a bed to share. He looked toward the cabin where he knew his brother was sleeping with his beloved. How had he ever thought to make a marriage arrangement like his work in such close quarters? Then he knew that he had not counted on falling in love with his wife. Never having really been in love, how could he have known the drive to be with one's mate that God had molded into his mortal flesh? He only knew he could not continue this way.

∞∞∞

Christmas morning all the family men sported new buckskin shirts, made for the winter, as they tucked into a hearty breakfast. The excited shouts of laughter from the children as they competed to spy the pickle nestled high in the camp tree added to the merry mood. Runwell cajoled tasty scraps from one and all. Then came the flurry of gifts passed one to another.

"Thank you!" Gray exclaimed as he turned a hunting knife, with an intricately carved wooden handle, over and over in his hand.

"I had Charles carve it, he is the craftsman," Jacob explained. "Use it wisely."

"Of course," Gray assured him.

Carrie showed off the beautiful cradle her beloved designed for their firstborn. Then she marveled at the artistry of Sara's gift.

"What an ingenious idea, a "Journey Quilt." Carrie inspected the scenes of their journey depicted on the soft cloth through Sarah's delicate stitches.

Sarah felt a pang of guilt as she sat with the beautifully worked wedding ring quilt that Cordelia had made for her and Jacob. Did she not suspect that sharing a bed might not be in their future?

"Thank-you for the lovely shawl. You do have a gift for needle-work." Cordelia sat down beside Sarah.

"Your quilt is a very beautiful," Sarah smoothed her hand over the soft folds.

"For a beautiful couple, my dear." Cordelia twisted on the tree stump seat to look at her directly. "Make good use of it," she said with a wink.

Chapter 16

The next week was spent readying the cabin for when the real cold weather set in. Provisions were laid in the cabin on makeshift board shelves surrounding a mud daubed fireplace. A bedframe from the old home topped with a fluffy feather ticking mattress and soft linens filled one side of the room. A crudely built table stood beside the bed. A good supply of candles lay on top beside several kerosene lamps and hanging lanterns.

Charles and Carrie spent the nights after Christmas in the cabin as a belated honeymoon. Late in the afternoon, on New Year's Eve, Carrie and Sarah returned with bundles of freshly laundered linens to redress the bed. Sarah noted the glow in her sister's cheeks and teased her mercilessly as the sheets were tucked into place.

"New Year's Eve...a good day for new beginnings," Carrie declared as she patted the bedding into a neat, smooth finish.

"Hmm," Sarah agreed, half-heartedly. She was no closer to a declaration to Jacob for a fresh start. She turned to check the inventory of provisions.

"You haven't told him, have you?" Carrie asked

with discernable frustration.

"I haven't found the right time," Sarah defended.

"Guess I'll have to take matters into my own hands," Carrie shot back with a direct glare and a dare.

"You most certainly will not."

"I will, if I do not see you two in each other's arms immediately."

"I will, I will. Just give me time."

"Today. Start the New Year right."

Sarah felt the walls of the small space closing in under her sister's scrutiny. She left the cabin. Carrie could finish organizing the contents of the other bundles. As she wandered the walking paths in the nearby woods, she racked her brain for an idea of how to start such an intimate conversation with her beloved.

"About time we call it a day...losin' the light. New Year's Eve, the cabin is all yours, brother. What do you say?" Charles teased.

"Nah, you two enjoy another night," Jacob deflected, putting away the tools.

"No, it's a good day to make a new resolution to start your marriage off on new footing."

"I'll have to pass today, but thanks," Jacob moved toward the campsite.

Charles blocked his path. "You haven't talked to her, have you?"

"Just haven't found the right time."

"There is no right time. Just plant yourself in front of her and declare you can't take it anymore. She is driving you to distraction and she must understand a man has needs!"

Jacob snorted. "Is that how you won your bride?"

"Yup. After I won her that cow. She fairly swooned."

"Sarah is not likely to swoon. She is likely to take a frypan to my head."

Charles sobered. "Well...you can't know until you try. Sooner the better."

∞∞∞

The conversation at supper was subdued.

Charles finally excused himself. "I'm going to check the wagon, see if the mend is holding. Jacob would you go get a lantern from the cabin and give me a hand."

"Sure, be right there." Jacob stood and gave Sarah a long look before turning to go.

Sarah warmed from the top of her head down to her toes. He could ask her anything at that moment and yes would be the answer. She was shocked at her own thoughts.

Cordelia interrupted her heated musing. "Sarah, would you go to the cabin and get about two pounds of beans for me? I'd like to soak them overnight."

"Yes," hurrying out the door, Sarah was glad to have a task to distract her.

As she entered the cabin, she saw Jacob rummaging on the shelves in the half light. "The lanterns are over by the fireplace."

Jacob felt around to find the lantern and the matches. He soon had a soft light illuminating the room.

"Cordelia sent me to get some beans. She wants to soak them overnight." She located a large bowl. As he held a sack open for her to dip the required amount, the door slammed shut and the latch bolted.

Hey, who's out there?" Jacob yelled.

He heard the mirthful voices of Carrie and Charles taunting at the same time, "You two can stay in there until you talk to each other and stop this dancing around."

"Sarah, you tell Jacob what you told me. No more pussyfooting around. We can't stand watching you two lovebirds torture yourselves," Carrie giggled. Then the laughter faded as the two moved away from the cabin.

∞∞∞

Jacob tried the door. It was securely bolted from the outside.

"Sarah?"

He could hear her fumbling in the dim light. Then a single candle flared, illuminating where she stood by the fireplace. He moved toward her. She skittered out of the light. He picked up the candle and followed her the short distance to find her backed up to the bed. In the small space there was nowhere else to go.

"Sarah, what is this about?" His voice rumbled huskily above her head.

"I don't know, some kind of prank?"

"What did Carrie mean? Do you have something to tell me?"

"I-I don't know what she is talking about."

Jacob looked beyond his love to the bed. "Is this the quilt Mama made for you?"

Sarah turned, surprised to see that it was. There was also a pure white nightdress laid at the foot of the bed.

"Sarah?" Jacob was waiting for her answer.

"I did not lay out this quilt or this gown," Sarah turned back to explain. "Maybe Carrie did? I am sorry if my sister's actions have given you any discomfort. I may have spoken out of turn to her concerning...concerning my feelings..."

"Your feelings?" he repeated.

"Jacob, I cannot continue as we have been," the words rushed out of Sarah's mouth.

"Meaning?" he coaxed, hoping he understood.

"I –I want us to be closer," she whispered, her head bowed.

The silence grew in the close quarters as he considered her words. He couldn't take his eyes off his beautiful Sarah. Then he realized his silence had shaken her, as he heard a soft sob escape her lips. He stepped forward and gathered her small hands in his large ones and reached to tip her chin to look into her eyes, misted with tears. "That is my wish as well."

"I am sorry. I know I am being too bold. I should have waited for you to speak..." Sarah rushed on as if she did not hear his words, he silenced her nervous chatter with his hand. Then he covered her mouth with his in a soft kiss. Her response sealed his decision that tonight their marriage would be made complete.

Tears filled her eyes as she turned her back to him to brush her fingers over the gown and noticed her mother's lace stitched along the neckline. A small note in Carrie's handwriting lay among the folds. "For a beautiful bride. I wish you and Jacob the same happiness and passion I have found with my Charles."

Jacob placed his hands gently on her shoulders and leaned into her back to place a soft kiss on the top of her head. He waited silently for a response. Sarah knew it was time. No more waiting. She reached to pull her hair away from the top of her blouse. Jacob accepted her signal and moved his fingers to help her with the tiny buttons down the back of her dress. He pressed his lips along her back, following his hands downward, as the garment parted. Sarah shivered with the rush of cool air and the brush of his lips on her skin. As her dress pooled to the floor around her feet, he lifted the fine gown down over her head as she slipped her crude shift off her shoulders, dropping it to her feet. He touched his lips softly along her neck as he slowly pulled his ribbon from her hair, letting golden waves cascade down her back. The feel of his fingertips brushing along as he arranged her hair filled her with joy. At last she would be his true bride.

Jacob stared at his beautiful bride, a gift from God. Her curls spilled down her shoulders like a golden mantle. She turned to face him. She answered by silently helping him with his buttons and laces. Her fingers trembled as she prepared him as he had done for her. When she was done, he lifted her onto the bed and joined her to complete the vows made months before. His breath caught as he realized that all the years of waiting had been for this moment when he could give himself to his bride, clean and whole, not burdened with jaded thoughts and memories. Only she would fill his senses with the delights of this intimate ritual. He gently caressed her smooth bare shoulder with his work-roughened hand. He exhaled, his breath ruffling the delicate lace on the bodice of her gown as he bent to press a kiss where his hand had lighted, then his finger slowly traced the curve of her arm downward until he clasped her hand, pausing to give her one more moment to be sure.

Chapter 17

Bitter cold rushed in with a January "blue norther". The company hunkered down in their fortified tents and hastily built cabins to wait out the raw North Texas winter. As predicted, travel between campsites became nearly impossible, trips to town on the road completely so.

"Here is another wrap, dear." Cordelia laid a thin square of plaid wool cloth onto Carrie's shoulders. "I can't remember it being this cold back home."

"Don't think it ever was." Charles added a log to the fire. The ladies were all huddled around the heat, the men rested against the wall on makeshift mats of quilts unloaded from the wagon.

The door slammed open and in stumbled Gray. "Come, see the snow!"

The group roused, stepping out of the dimly lit cabin into blinding white daylight. Giant, fat flakes of fluffy snow were fast covering the landscape. For the sojourners from the deep South the sight was rare and delightful.

Gray and the men went right to work building snow cannon balls and firing them at one another in a rivalrous flurry. The women stepped cautiously along, fingering the soft icing on the bushes. The beauty of the whitewashed wilderness belied the destruction that could follow if the storm was too generous in its gift.

As the day wore on the camp came to life. Those brave enough to come out organized a full-on snow war complete with rival forts and tactical strategies intended to defeat the enemy.

Cordelia shook her head at the mayhem. "Strange how men who just shot to kill can now play at war with such abandon."

"Defies all reason but it's in their nature, I guess." Sarah ducked as an errant missile grazed her head.

"Hot coffee's ready," Carrie came up and yelled to the warriors. They reluctantly shut down the fight to come shuffle around the bonfire that had been started as the snow party progressed.

"Didn't see this in Mississip did ya?" Eli stomped up red-faced from exertion.

"No indeed. God can make a spectacle of even a winter storm." Cordelia smiled, offering him a warm cup to wrap his hands around.

After the battlers got a second wind provided by the warm refreshment, the war resumed. With snow-fire flying all around the women planned a makeshift lunch menu to cook for all the revelers. The day ended with everyone cold on the outside but warmed within by the good food and fellowship.

∞∞∞

The days of unrelenting cold began to take their toll. Another more severe ice storm bent the trees until they snapped. Tents not fortified with lean-to roofs collapsed. Misery and sickness spread through the camp.

"Mattie Blalock's got the grippe," Jacob noted. He sat beside Sarah's chair as she worked on a mend in his winter coat.

"Hope she'll fight it off, Eli would be lost without her. But at her age it'll be tit for tat. She's a strong woman but these conditions will try us all I'm afraid," Cordelia sighed.

"I heard a child over in the German train died day before yesterday. They are blaming the cold and damp for the inflammation in his lungs," Sarah added the sad news.

"It's been sleeting for 24 hours. When will it stop?" Carrie stared at the dwindling fire, murmuring more to herself than to the company.

"How many dead does that make so far?" Sarah questioned.

"Three at the last count. I hope the fever the Carters had will not spread." Cordelia got up to poke the fire back to life.

Carrie wrapped her arms tighter around her growing middle and stared at the scattering sparks as Cordelia prodded the flame.

"The rider who came out from town last week says this is the roughest winter he can remember." Charles reached over to tuck the blanket tighter around Carrie's feet.

"I refuse to lay the unfortunate weather upon God's providence." Sarah's pronouncement reminded the family that some in the camp had begun to curse the day they left their homes to embark on this foolhardy trip.

"Some folks are just wrung out and cannot take any more setbacks." Cordelia came to the defense of those not as tough-minded as her own brood.

"I know, I just feel like railing at God at times too, and I must check myself as He has also given me all of you." Sarah panned her gaze around to all her now blended and loved family, landing on her beloved Jacob.

Jacob pulled her down to the mat alongside himself and brushed a kiss over her temple. He felt the rush of need for her. In the confines of the shared space, they had not been alone together again since New Year's week. Charles and Carrie shared the soft bed. Cordelia had the double mattress on the other side of the fireplace intended for a new bed when they reached their new home. Gray was spending more time sharing accommodations with his friends, an arrangement Jacob thought suspect but had not had time to investigate. His days were taken up with hunting for game and keeping the woodpile replenished which distracted thoughts of his personal needs. He was frustrated but content to just hold Sarah close against him, at last, as they slept on the mats by the fire each night.

∞ ∞ ∞

Aloud banging at the door roused them all from sleep. Jacob rose to answer.

"Please come, Mattie's turned for the worse. I need Cordelia to give her some of her remedy." Eli shook with emotion, battling the tears welling in his wide eyes.

Cordelia went straight for her medicine bag filled with natural remedies.

"I'll come too." Sarah gathered cloths and a blanket, paltry items to do battle with death in this wilderness. Running through the cruel storm Sarah spoke her plea aloud to God for stamina, wisdom and healing for Mattie.

The pallor of death was already washing Mattie's face, her harsh gasps for breath agonizingly loud in the otherwise silent cabin. Cordelia and Sarah got right to work. Cordelia prepared a plaster of herbs, pulled from her bag, to apply to Mattie's chest and then prepared a tincture to drop into her mouth to calm her. Soon her labored breathing had changed to the slow, shallow rhythm indicating that this was a battle they were going to lose.

Sarah reached beneath the blankets and felt the ice-cold flesh, already losing the warmth of life. "She is growing cold. We are losing her aren't we."

"I am afraid all I can do now is make her comfortable with a sedating herb. She will go peacefully if I can manage it." Cordelia's eyes welled as she repositioned the blankets in a useless gesture to forestall the inevitable cooling preceding death.

Feeling the need to do something to mark this monumental passage that all must make with more than silence, Sarah began to hum the hymns detailing heavens delights as she ministered the small physical comforts she could. Cordelia joined in and together they provided an accompaniment for Mattie's home-going later in the afternoon.

In her last moment, Mattie briefly opened her eyes and turned her head to smile at each of them as if she found comfort in the music, then she breathed her last.

∞∞∞

Jacob slammed the sharp edge of the shovel as hard as he could at the frozen ground to only make a small dent. The men dug twelve graves in the past fourteen days and the dying did not seem to be abating.

"I can't believe Johnny is gone." Charles came up from his work down the row. "He made it all the way through the war to give it up to lung fever here?" He shook his head as he surveyed the cold field of fresh graves. Strangers, friends and loved ones were to be left behind in unfamiliar land, like in the hasty resting places of the warriors of the South.

"Makes you feel like the devil's chasin' us, doesn't it?" Jacob gave the earth another jab.

"Why Johnny and not that good for nothin' Prior and his gang?" Charles grumbled as he joined in Jacob's assault on the newest hole.

"Yeah, it's hard not to question God right about now. I can hardly stand to see Eli so low. He took Mattie's passing real hard. They'd been together for 40 years."

"I just want to get movin' again. I want my son to be born in our new home."

"A son is it, could be a girl."

"Well, she will need sweet air to breath, not the stench of death in this place."

"Better dig faster, the service is at two."

The two slashed at the hard dirt for another hour, then slogged to the cabin to change.

∞ ∞ ∞

At the appointed time the line of mourners snaked behind the wagons carrying two plain wooden caskets to the muddy field where the grave sites were prepared. Eli trudged behind Mattie as she was carried to her final resting place, his giant shoulders heaving with grief. The party laid the two caskets into the ground and sang a mournful good-bye that echoed back from the surrounding forest in nature's own sad refrain of cruel winter wind swaying the treetops.

Jacob and Charles stood on either side of Eli as

he cast the first earth into the dank hole. "I'm goin' back home, Mattie. I can't go ahead without you."

Charles and Jacob added their handful of dirt and turned to escort Eli back to the camp.

"You can't mean that, Eli," Jacob probed quietly.

"I do." Eli moved ahead of the brothers.

"What about the others. They are counting on you to lead us to the Big Valley. You are the only one that knows the way." Jacob caught up.

"I'll make sure you know the way—you are my second. I trust you to finish the trip."

"Eli, what have you got back home but spent land and government regulators. Mattie's buried here in Texas. The dream you both shared will die with her if you turn back now. And what about your sister waitin' for you?" Jacob continued.

"I know you are right, but I have to have some time to think it over. I just can't see my way now that she's gone." Eli stopped and squeezed his eyes to pinch the flow of tears.

The three men stood silent and waited for the wave of grief to pass.

The days grew steadily warmer as winter slinked away driven by spring's renewing power. Buds unfurled on tree and brush, tender sprouts struggled through the crusted mud, promising a glorious show, in time.

"Glad you changed your mind about leaving us." Jacob clapped Eli on the back as he came up to the wagon to plot the route to Fort Worth.

"Well you are right about back home. Workin' my-self to death on the Texas frontier doesn't seem as foreboding as bein' regulated to death back home," Eli quipped. "Besides, Mattie would've boxed my ears off if I gave up now."

"True words, brother." Charles grinned at the thought of Mattie taking Eli to task.

"Road is hardly fit for travel, but I feel the folks are gettin' restless so it's the mud or the infernal complainin' and I choose the former." Eli unrolled a crudely drawn map detailing the trail ahead, watering and camp sites noted. "I hear they had one of the best growin' seasons last year, got top price per bushel for wheat and cotton. Hope we can do as well. It would go far toward our getting a good foothold here."

"What about the Indians out in the territories?" Jacob asked, having heard of their raiding in past years.

"Well, my sister claims they have settled down quite a bit. You hear of a raid now and then, but they go for the livestock mainly. No life lost recently. But now the war is over, a lot of the troops have been recalled back East, so it is a concern we'll have to take into account."

"Well, I've seen the whites of the Yanks' eyes so I think I can deal with the enemy here in like manner," Charles offered with bravado.

The men spent the early afternoon discussing

the details of getting the train rolling again. They were determined to move out in two days.

∞∞∞∞

"Dogwood's in bloom." Sarah shared the news of the first harbinger of spring with Jacob as she returned from her trip for fresh water.

"I'd like to see that." Jacob gave her a sideways glance from his stooped position over the chopping block, ax positioned for another split in the log balanced on top. His clearly readable expression suggested they might grab a moment for a walk alone.

Sarah responded to his silent invitation with pleasure. "I could prepare a lunch." She turned her back and poured the water from the pail into the tub of dirty breakfast dishes, then looked back to receive his answer.

"Soon as I finish this pile of wood." His intense stare sent a frisson of anticipation through her.

"And I, these dishes and our lunch." She answered as casually as she could. It had been so long since they had been alone to even talk. She spent the next hours with her chores and a building excitement that she would have Jacob to herself for an afternoon.

It was warm and the woods were bursting with signs of spring. Sarah led Jacob along the stream that fed the lake until they came to a small clearing. There, they saw the lone tree standing at the edge of the thicket, bedecked, as a bride, with delicate white blooms. They crossed the clearing and laid their lunch out on an old soft quilt. They talked of dreams for their new life as they ate. The breeze carried new scents, Texas scents and hope, Texas hope.

"I hope for a clearing such as this, the river on one side and pasture on the other. Fields of wheat and —whatever grows best in Texas." Jacob swept his arm across the view, sandwich in hand.

"And a cabin with two rooms and maybe a loft, room to grow," Sarah continued his muse then blushed at the obvious meaning her words implied.

Jacob turned to her, his intent clear. He took her gently in his arms and kissed her deeply. "Sarah, I love you as my own heart and I am so grateful you came with me."

"As am I," Sarah responded as she offered her kiss in thanks for his invitation to create a new life from one so broken.

There, under the white bower, secluded from view, they celebrated their love again. This time it was with the slow deliberateness of comfortable lovers.

Chapter 18

The wagons lined up along the road facing west. There was a flurry of last-minute packing to be done before pulling out. It was a challenge to get the new cradle and trunk loaded.

Sarah brushed her fingers along the rough wood planks inside the empty one-room cabin that had been their home for the past three months. Inside these walls the two families were knit into one. It held other memories for her. In this crude place her love for Jacob was sealed and she would remember it always as a place of delight.

"Come dear, time to load up." Cordelia peeked in the door.

Sarah went out to face the future as a Texas frontier pioneer.

Travel was difficult due to the road conditions, but Jacob was glad to be moving again. The women walked ahead in groups, gaggling excitedly about new homes and gardens. The men took turns driving the wagons, then riding point and alongside the perimeter rounding up wayward children and livestock. The lightly wooded countryside was pristine compared to that of the scorched lands of Mississippi and the rugged forests of Arkansas.

Jacob heard the stories of the peaceful Caddo who lived in the North Texas woodlands for centuries. None could doubt why, the land was fertile and full of game. This land was already claimed so they had to pass it up for the uncertainty out in the territories past Fort Worth. Nevertheless, he felt renewal with each mile forward.

He enjoyed riding point, with Runwell taking the lead. He could see the land first, before the others, and reflect on past and future in solitude. The deep sorrow of the past was washed clean by the vision of a future with his new family in this land of promise. He mused again on how his feelings must reflect those of God's own chosen people as they moved into the land of milk and honey. Dangers awaited but the lure of the land's bounty urged them on.

"Jake, got a problem." Eli rode up, interrupting his musing.

"What's that?" Jacob turned in the saddle to answer.

"Seems some of the youngin's have up and left with Prior Mullens and his gang. Families been lookin' for them all mornin' and they are definitely not with the train." Eli frowned in concern.

"Who's missing?" Jacob hated to ask because he dreaded the answer.

"Well we can't find my James and your Gray, J. D. Greer and Sam Stovall. And of course, Mary Jane admitted she ain't seen Prior for at least 48 hours, about a day before we left. We thought James was with Gray. Sarah said you all thought Gray was with James, so we didn't miss them 'til the noon meal."

"You got an idea where they might be headed to?" Jacob already knew the task before him, to go reclaim the boys from the outlaws.

"Mary Jane said something about Prior's interest in Jefferson. It's a growin' town and there's a lot of nefarious dealin's to interest a gang of outlaws like Prior and his men." Eli spat to highlight his disgust.

"You know I've got to go after them," Jacob returned.

"I can manage the train. Take some men with you. It could get ugly when you corner that rat."

The two men turned their horses back to the train and rode in silence, each wrapped in thoughts of their wayward loved ones and the danger they faced.

∞∞∞

Sarah rushed to greet Jacob as he rode into the hastily made camp. "I am so afraid for Gray." Sarah folded into Jacob's embrace.

"I'm goin' to get him back. They cannot be far." Jacob stroked Sarah's hair as she nestled into his chest.

"I had no idea he had any attachment to that layabout." Sarah detached herself to pace.

"I did, and let it go," Jacob confessed.

Sarah stopped to stare at him with accusation

flashing in her eyes. "Did you now?"

"I caught him several times with James and some of the other boys gambling back home and outside the camp since we left. I talked to him about it and thought he and I had an agreement that he would stay away from Prior. I never thought he would leave like this." Jacob could feel the sensation of daggers from her glare piercing his heart. He had kept something from her; lied by omission.

"Why didn't you tell me?" Sarah hissed quietly.

"I thought I could gain his trust by keeping quiet and maybe help you with his raising. He needs a man to guide him now Sarah," Jacob offered his paltry excuse knowing it was not good enough for the sin committed.

"If something happens to him…," Sarah turned to cover the tears leaving the last words to Jacob's imagination…, "*I will never forgive you.*"

He quickly gathered supplies and, with nothing more to say, mounted his horse and rode away.

Sarah could not turn back to face him. She knew if something happened to Gray, she would never forgive herself. She had been so wrapped up in her new life, the rigors of the trail, her relationship with Jacob and his family that she had allowed Gray to drift in and out, no questions asked. Jacob was right. She thought it many times before, that Gray needed a good man to emulate…a good man like Jacob.

∞ ∞ ∞

Jacob rode up to Eli's wagon where Charles and two men, fathers of the other two boys, were waiting.

"Talked with Mary Jane and she thinks Prior was in fact plannin' to go to Jefferson. Here's a map to get you south through what used to be Caddo land." Eli spread the hand drawn directions out for the men to see. "Shouldn't have any trouble along the way, the route is frequently traveled."

The men rode south on the old Caddo road soon coming into the denser forests of the upper East Texas thicket. There were indeed travelers along the way headed to the major river-port city of Jefferson. Jacob inquired whether Prior's party had been spotted as they passed the slower wagons loaded with goods to be transported down the river to the gulf and beyond. He finally got confirmation of a sighting. At least they were on the right trail.

Two days later they rode into the bustling commercial hub of North-East Texas. The riverfront town boasted over 5,000 inhabitants so the men knew the task before them would be difficult.

"Knowing Prior's habits, I suspect we should start with the dance halls and gambling Hells. I'm sure there are plenty to choose from. I say we split up and meet back this evening to compare our findings and plan from there," Jacob suggested in the form of an order and the men agreed.

Charles and Jacob turned south down the main street as the other two men turned north. They spent the remainder of the day pretending to drink, in first one saloon after another, chatting up the loose-tongued customers until they finally hit paydirt.

"Yep, I seen 'em this mornin' goin' into the back room. They've got a big game goin' on back there and these sodbusters are goin' in pumped full of liquor-fueled bravado and comin' out with the devil chasin' their tail." The rumpled old gentleman chuckled at the gullible rubes plight.

"How long these games usually go on? I'm feelin' lucky today," Charles inquired.

"Last one went on for twenty-four hours before the clientele got rowdy and old Grover over there put a stop to it."

Jacob gave a nod to the bartender who looked up at the mention of his name. "He the owner?"

"Yep, looks the other way when boys like the ones you're huntin' come into town to do some business, unless it attracts too much attention and gets the law pokin' around."

Jacob stood and motioned for Charles to follow. "Thanks for the tip." He laid a coin on the table and put his finger to his lips to indicate the drink it would buy would also buy the tipster's silence.

The group met back at the hotel to formulate a plan.

"I think we should get the law involved," Ben Stovall argued.

"Why? These rats have done nothing criminal, yet. I say we stake out the place and follow them out when they're done and surprise them," Jacob laid out his plan.

"And if our boys don't want to come with us?"

Charles voiced the very real concern of all the men.

"That's a chance we take, and we can't make them come back if they are determined to follow these curs to perdition," Jacob voiced the hard truth. The boys were of age and could not be compelled to return.

∞ ∞ ∞

After dark the men took separate routes to the tavern and staked out all the doors. Charles went back in to establish the game was still in progress and then all they could do was wait. At about four the next morning the gamesters spilled into the street in a brawl. Jacob and Charles held their places as the violence unfolded. The fathers of the other two boys rounded the corners from the back of the building, guns drawn but cautious. They each sighted their boy in the fray. The grown men were getting the best of the boys while the rest of the crowd was ramping up the fight into a life and death situation. Suddenly a cry rang out from the center of the melee. Hardened men recently returned from the war recognized the agonized sound of surprise from one grievously wounded. The crowd briefly opened to reveal one of Prior's men clutching his bloodied shirt, a Bowie knife lodged, handle deep, in his chest. Then the fight turned deadly serious as guns were drawn and shots rang out. The crowd scattered, but not before three were gunned down. Jacob and Charles looked on in horror as they realized one was Gray, another Sam Stovall. Prior's gang clambered onto their horses and galloped away, leaving the rest of the gamers scrambling for cover and a place to hide from the law that was racing down the street toward then.

James Blalock scrambled to Gray, shaking him and screaming with rage. Jacob and Charles ran to Gray's side. He was still breathing; his wound was not fatal. The guttural growl rising into a primal shout from across the street indicated Ben Stovall had not determined the same for his son.

"I'm following them," Levi Greer raced up to inform them. "J. D.'s gone with them."

"Wait Levi, let the sheriff take care of it." Jacob reached up to grab Levi's arm to restrain him.

"No, they'll get away and we won't know what direction they took. I can't go back to Maude without him." Levi yanked his arm free and raced to get his horse.

Jacob knew this time would come, a reckoning with Prior was his fate. He nodded toward Gray. "Take care of him for me, Charles, for Sarah." He retrieved his horse and followed Levi.

Jacob and Levi rode hard behind the escaping outlaws. The gang had been a nuisance until now but after this night's work they owed for lives lost and would face a noose. Jacob had seen enough of violence in the war and wanted no part of this fight with Prior, but he had to put an end to the deserter's influence on those he cared for. He left the road and crashed through the thick underbrush into the forest. His mount dodged the obstacle course of closely standing pines. Jacob's mind shifted into battle mode. The terrain was eerily like that of the Tennessee forests he fought in for four long years. The blood rushed in his ears as he braced for combat. Careening into a clearing, he reigned up as he came to a jetty surrounded by the river. The men ahead had dismounted leaving their horses skittering to get away from the water.

"J. D. come on out here," Levi broke into the clearing behind him and hollered for his son.

"You want your little nit, let us ride out and you can have him," Prior yelled back from the cover of the trees.

"How do we know he's with you?" Jacob spun his horse around to the direction from which he thought Prior's call came.

"Squeal you little hog farmer," Prior taunted as a cry of pain rang out from J. D.

"You let him be," Levi returned, more agitated by the minute.

"Take it easy, Levi," Jacob warned quietly, as he motioned to the area in which he thought Prior was holed up. Then on Jacob's signal they charged forward into the tree line, coming off their horses as they flew by the hidden men, each rolling a man as J.D. broke free and tackled the third. Stray shots rang out, pinging off the pine bark as the scuffle intensified but soon the battle-hardened vets had the deserters down and disarmed.

"Now get up you trash and start walking," Jacob hissed into Prior's ear. "You are never going to meddle with my family again."

Jacob and Levi, doubled up with J. D., rode back into town leading Prior and two of his men on foot and trussed like turkeys. After delivering them to the sheriff they made their way to find Gray.

The doctor worked with quiet efficiency to draw the bullet from Gray's shoulder and tend the fight wounds of the boys.

"Sam's dead isn't he," James stated flatly, not looking up from his wounded hand as he worried a loose piece of bandage.

"Yes," Jacob replied without elaboration.

"I tried to get them to go back to the train. Prior was usin' us like slaves, workin' us, makin' us do his biddin'. I knew he wasn't goin' to let us in on the take. We were just dumb youngins' hangin' on his coat-tails." James swiped at the stream leaking from the corner of his eye.

Jacob placed his hand on the trembling boy's shoulder. "We all get gulled sometimes, son. The main thing is that we learn from our mistakes. You've got a fine father who needs you to help him follow your mother's dream. You up for that adventure?"

"Yes Sir." James looked up to meet Jacob's eyes. He had grown older and wiser in a few days time.

∞ ∞ ∞

Gray lay in the grip of fever. Jacob and Charles took shifts watching over him. On the second day, while rummaging through the boy's sparsely packed cloth sack, Jacob found a letter from William, one of Gray's brothers. He read it, feeling like an eavesdropper on a private lecture.

Camps near Dalton, Ga. April 24th, 1864

> *Gray,*
> *Dear brother, I write you a few lines which will inform you that I am well and I trust they will find you well and all right. Gray I learned from Frankey's letter that Prior Mullens was at Mary Jane's. I want to say a few words to you in the way of advice concerning him though I hope you may be acting prudent. I feel it my duty to warn you to have nothing to do with him. Don't countenance him in any way whatever for he is a worthless, trifling fellow, a deserter and a foresworn man. If he is ever brought back here it is the opinion he will be shot which would be nothing more than he deserves for his was willful desertion at a time too when every man was needed and should have stood square up to his post. It vexes me to hear of him being back there for there is nothing that is too mean for him to do. I don't want you all to countenance him in any way nor suffer him to come on the place. He would not lie around Mary Jane's if I was there for he knows that I know how low down he is. I don't think he would face me at all. I am sorry for Mary Jane and I am surprised to think that she will suffer him and his colleagues to lay around her knowing at the same time that he is disgracing her and eating up her living. Besides, it is causing people to lose all confidence in her and of course*

no one will assist her if she will suffer such trash to stay about her. I am surprised she has no better sense but if not it can't be helped. I hope you will take the warning I have given you and have nothing to do with such people. I want you to live honorable and respectable in this world. I hope you consider these things well and act accordingly.

Your brother until death, William Partin

Read the above lines to yourself and no feelings will be hurt.

"Should have taken heed to him," Gray whispered hoarsely as he emerged from his long sleep to find Jacob sitting with his letter from William in his hand.

"Gray, thank God!" Jacob stood and bent over the bed.

"What happened, how long have I been here?"

Jacob gave Gray the details as the boy slammed his balled fist on the mattress with anguish. There could be no secrets between them now. He had to talk straight to try to get Gray set back on the right path.

"William warned me, I just wanted to be my own boss," Gray motioned to the letter.

"I shouldn't have read your private mail," Jacob apologized.

"You tried to warn me too. You and William would have gotten along. You both want to tell me what to do."

"He just wanted what is best for you and so do I. I would like to be your friend and a brother if you'll let me."

"You came all this way to get me," Gray stated a matter of fact.

"Sarah and Carrie are depending on you to carry on the Partin name, as they are McKennas now. Can't let anything happen to you," Jacob grinned.

Gray mustered a slight smile and nodded.

"You going to be ready to go back to the train with me then?" Jacob inquired gently.

"I will—brother," Gray answered then slipped back into a restful sleep.

Chapter 19

Sarah struggled to handle the six oxen pulling the five-ton wagon. Gray usually walked beside the wagon commanding the cattle easily by yanking the jerk line to keep the beasts on track. Sarah sat on the jockey box atop the wagon front, feeling safer aboard the wagon than on the ground. It took all her concentration to manage the leads that controlled the animals.

The hard board seat rattled her to her bones. Jacob had been gone for days. The mantle of fear she wore during the war years returned to sit heavily on her shoulders. Would the men return, the new men God had provided to people her life?

Now, three women were journeying into a hostile land alone just as Naomi returned to Israel with her two daughters-in-law. Sarah had faith God would provide; but the fear threatened to overwhelm her courage.

"Winds kickin' up," Eli rode up and yelled to Sarah, as he held onto his hat in the increasingly strong gusts. "We're pullin' up and makin' camp soon, so watch the front wagons and listen for the signal. Looks like we're gonna' have some weather, so battin' down."

Sarah nodded acknowledgment of the warning. When the signal came, she gee and hawed the oxen into position in the circle. Cordelia and Carrie helped to tie down the site more securely than usual, as the wind grew more aggressive. The sky was black and menacing, taking on a greenish hue just before the mantle of heaven tore open and released its torrent of hard stinging rain.

The women crouched in the wagon box crowded in among their belongings, protected from the maelstrom only by the flapping canvas bonnet.

"Father, preserve us in the raging storm, protect our cattle and possessions from destruction, forgive us any trespasses if this day should be the last number of our days,..." Cordelia began to pray aloud as the lightening began to strike immediately around the camp, sizzling and crackling through the trees. They could hear branches tearing from their anchors on the boughs. Just as they thought it could not get worse, the first ice ball from heaven's cannon tore through the bonnet and struck the trunk between them.

"We have to get under the box," Cordelia yelled. "The hail is too big for the bonnet to hold. Hurry." She clambered out the back opening and slid under the wagon box into the mud below. Sarah and Carrie followed, the cold rain and hail pelted them as they escaped. They clung to one another as the storm raged on for another half hour.

When the sky began to clear, the battered travelers emerged from their hiding places to assess the damage. The camp was covered with forest debris and large hail. Trees were broken and uprooted all around. Animals lay injured on the ice-covered ground. As the men walked among them dispatching those that could not be saved, a wail went up from women and children to see the loss. Sarah walked away from the camp and lifted her eyes to the clearing heavens that had just rained such destruction. She could not formulate a retort, just a silent, weary, "God why? Jacob, where are you, I need you. I cannot go on alone."

Jacob and the returning party hunkered in the underbrush as the storm pelted the upper branches of the tall pines. Limbs and debris fell all around as the storm clawed the forest like a wild animal looking for hidden prey. He worried about Sarah and the women back at the train. Had the storm stalked them as well? It was coming from their general direction. He needed to get back to her, to make amends with the return of Gray, safe, if not completely sound. He strained with frustration at the storm's delay. As the winds began to die down, he urged the group to remount and pick their way through the debris on the road until they came to a stream that had become a raging torrent. They could go no further.

"I know you are in a rush to get back, but Eli will take care of the women." Charles pulled up by Jacob and surveyed the roiling water in what should have been a peacefully trickling stream.

"I know but what must Sarah and Carrie be thinking? They must be worried sick about Gray. And Carrie due for her confinement soon, she must be needing you," Jacob turned a worried look toward Charles.

"And Sarah needs you too, brother."

"Don't know about that. You should have seen her face when I told I knew about Gray's dealings with Prior. I don't know if she can forgive that betrayal of her trust. I took it upon myself to meddle in her family affairs without her permission, in fact against her express wishes and I don't know if she can forget that." Jacob turned back to stare at the torrent.

"She loves you Jacob, and she will forgive. You were trying to help, to take a load off her shoulders. She will understand." Charles shifted in his saddle, fidgeting as a former soldier not used to making sentimental pronouncements.

"Well, we'll see, brother." Jacob turned his horse and picked back toward a clearing he had spotted earlier. "Come on boys, I saw a camp site a way back. We will stop for the night, give the water a chance to recede."

The women took inventory of their personal losses, then changed into dry clothes and set the site for the night. After eating a cold supper, Sarah wandered away from camp again. As she walked, Carrie came up by her side and wrapped an arm around her.

"You worried about the boys?"

"I am. Aren't you?" Sarah slowed to accommodate Carrie's awkward gait.

"Yes, but I know God has them in His hand."

"I know, but God has allowed us some fierce battles of late and I am weary as Job." Sarah stopped to look into her sister's eyes. There she saw a maturity she had not noticed before.

"Sarah, you have been a strength and a fortress for us all but now it is time to let go of that mantle. Let the rest of us carry our fair share. We are not alone now. We have Charles and Cordelia and Jacob."

"I don't know, I hurt Jacob with my accusations as he left. I can be a stubborn fool with wanting to be in control and I did not see Jacob was just trying to ease my burden. I am afraid he will be wary of me now. I need him so, it hurts."

"I know," Carrie smiled, indicating she felt the same for Charles. "And I know that Charles and Jacob will retrieve Gray and return safely and all will be well. Then you will see that Jacob loves you to distraction and a little spat will not change that."

"I pray so." Sarah returned her gaze to the clear, star filled sky to whisper, "I pray so."

They circled back into camp, coming upon Eli and Cordelia sharing a cup of coffee that Eli managed to prepare. He had gotten his fire to sputter to life. Sarah gave Carrie a nudge as they accepted a welcome cup of the warm brew.

Eli visited ever more frequently over the three months since Mattie's death. Sarah suspected Cordelia and Eli's mutual respect was headed for a more intimate understanding. She mused on the idea that frontier life made for formation of quick alliances. Folks could not easily survive alone so it was not unusual, or frowned upon, for widows or widowers to take on new partners quickly. She expected a declaration in the future but watched with amusement for the present.

Eli drew a crumpled piece of paper from his vest pocket. "Ladies, I am happy to inform you that this message arrived a short while ago by a rider headed on to Fort Worth. It is from our men." He handed the note to Sarah. "You will see that Gray and James and J.D. are retrieved injured but safe. I regret that Ben Stovall's boy, Jim, did not fare so well. He was killed in a street fight."

Sarah pressed her fingers to her mouth as she read the brief note. It concluded, *"Charles sends his love to Carrie. The boys send their apologies for their folly. With respect to all the connections till we meet again, Jacob McKenna."* No word for her. Jacob was truly angry at her for her scolding. Regret lay like a hot coal in her chest.

∞∞∞∞

Days on the now dusty trail turned to a week, then two, as the party pressed on toward the bustling settlement of Dallas. The newly incorporated town hugged the Trinity River and was purported to be the last place to outfit for settlement on the frontier further west. Sarah hated the idea of having to buy the coming year's supplies without Jacob's input, even though she was confident she could perform the task perfectly well. She never presumed to touch the stash of coins Jacob kept locked away in his trunk of personal items. She was reluctant to do so now, even though he had given her the key.

They left the pine forest and were now traveling through less densely covered timberland. The few settlements they encountered seemed prosperous, untouched by the recent struggle that scorched the entire south to wasteland. After months of viewing terrible destruction, these pristine lands were like coming into a new world.

"With lands like these, no threat would be so great to encourage me to leave," Carrie enthused as Sarah maneuvered the team forward.

"Not even the Indians said to roam the frontier we plan to claim?" Sarah teased her sister.

"No indeed, I will stand my ground once I get to it," Carrie shot back.

The train up ahead began to slow as riders raced back along the line to shout that they would be coming to a ridge soon and the traverse down into the plain would require strong handling and braking of the wagons.

Eli arrived just behind to offer his services to guide the McKennas' wagons down the treacherous slope. "Afternoon ladies, I believe you will need a stronger hand to get this wagon down to the plain so I will be back tomorrow morning to arrange that."

"We are much obliged to you Eli," Sarah thanked him respectfully although it grated that she knew she could not do it alone. Eli rode on back to the second wagon being handled by Cordelia and his conversation there was considerably longer.

"How long you think we will wait to hear their good news?" Carrie queried as she leaned back to the front from craning to watch the older couple.

"Can't be too much longer, they are turning heads and they know it so I think a wedding will be arranged in Dallas as soon as we arrive," Sarah predicted with amusement.

"Wish the men would get back soon to see that sight, else the shock of returning to find their mother swept up and Eli a member of the clan might be too much," Carrie laughed.

The wagons began to pull into a clearing to set camp for the night. All were too weary to attempt a descent this day. Campfires sprang to life, smells of coffee and cooking grease coiled through the camp, and music — harmonicas, fiddles, voices.

Just before supper a shout went out, "Who goes there?"

All quieted to hear the response.

"Jacob and Charles McKenna and party," Jacob's deep voice resonated through the camp and slammed into Sarah's heart.

He was here, at last.

∞ ∞ ∞

"Sarah, they've come!" Carrie raced clumsily toward the voices.

Sarah could not move, she was at once relieved and afraid, afraid to face Jacob. She could hear the greetings and accolades of the travelers as they welcomed the men back into the camp.

She stood and waited and then he was there, standing before her. The depth of her relief overwhelmed her, but she could not approach him. Those icy eyes that she had once feared, and then come to love, devoured her. Then he spoke.

"Can you forgive me?" Jacob asked.

"Forgive you?" she was confused, he was the injured party.

"I went behind your back in my dealings with Gray after you expressly told me not to, and for that I am deeply sorry." He approached to stand a breath away. She could feel the heat of him, smell the perfume that was his alone, dust, horse, and her beloved mate.

"But I was never angry with you, just myself, for missing the signs you so clearly saw. I could never forgive myself if anything happened to Gray." She folded into him, burying her head in his strong chest, her rock, her defender.

Jacob accepted his love, his life, into his arms and breathed a thank-you to God for his good fortune. He smoothed her hair with his hands as she pressed closer.

"I am relieved to hear it for I labored under the misapprehension that you would never forgive my interference." He smiled as he placed a soft kiss on the top of her bowed head.

"And I feared you would not forgive my shrewish scold." As she looked up, he caught her lips in a welcomed kiss.

"Alright you two, stand apart to greet our prodigal come home." Charles walked up escorting Gray who was still trussed in bandages.

Sarah disengaged from Jacob to embrace Gray then stood back to give him a stern look, "What were you thinking. We have been sick with worry."

"Well, I have not been thinking about anyone but myself. Jacob here has shown me the right of things and I must apologize for my disrespect." Gray turned a worshipful eye toward his brother-in-law.

Sarah realized that something had changed between Gray and Jacob, and it was a welcome revelation. She knew in that moment that she could give the guidance of her brother to manhood to her husband, a man worthy to be emulated. Another burden lifted from her.

Cordelia bustled up to gather the clan for supper. "Let's get these boys fed."

They all dispersed to the campfire for a hearty meal and a recounting of the sad adventure that led to one of their young traveler's untimely death.

Sarah noted Gray's contrite demeanor throughout the telling, as if he truly understood the folly of his rebellion. She reached to grasp his hand, "I am sorry you had to learn of Prior's character the hard way."

"Well sister, some of us are hard-headed and can learn in no other school but that of hard knocks. Least that's what Jacob said."

"Did he?" Sarah turned toward Jacob just as he rose and left the circle.

"Go after him, Sarah. He suffered much on your account and I wish his mind at ease," Charles quietly urged her to follow.

Sarah followed Jacob as he approached the ridge overlooking the vast plain to the west. As she came up beside him, he pulled her into his arms. They stood transfixed at the sight of the sunset, huge and brilliant in the Texas sky.

"There it is...our new home."

"It seems to go on forever."

"We will have to be strong to conquer such a land." Jacob turned to face her. "No more secrets, no more misunderstanding."

"Together in all things, a family." Sarah held his gaze.

"A family," he breathed as he bent to claim her lips against the magnificent backdrop of their promised land.

Chapter 20

Bacon sizzled in the pan; the aroma drew the family to the fire for breakfast. Eli strolled up beside Cordelia bearing his usual pot of strong coffee. They exchanged pleasant words, and lingering looks that were hard to miss by the newly arrived members. The group enjoyed lighthearted jesting and talk of the descent to the plain. It would be a harrowing day getting all the wagons down the steep path along the slope.

"Ah-hem," Eli got the groups attention. He was sitting unusually close to Cordelia, giving hint to what he was about to say. "Folks, your mother and I have an announcement to make. I know it will seem precipitous to you all, but we have come to an understanding. We are lookin' to get hitched in Dallas with or without your blessing."

The big man squirmed with discomfort before all the relations, but he continued. "Now just so you know, this is not a marriage of convenience only. I respect and love your mother, and she tells me she feels the same for this old codger, so we think we will make a good go of it." He paused to survey faces staring back, some amused, some shocked. "What say you?"

As the surprise wore off, the group responded

with laughter, and hearty backslapping, at the extra-ordinary news.

∞∞∞

"Did you know about this?" Jacob asked Sarah as she gathered utensils to wash and pack.

"Well, we suspected. Eli kept coming around at meals and paying us special attention when the train was on the move. We thought we detected a softening in Cordelia's reception of his attention. So, we are not surprised. How do you feel about it?"

"Well, once I get my wind back, I think I will be glad that my best friend and my mother will be as happy as I am." He pecked her cheek and headed off to finish his own chores to ready the wagon for the day.

"You think we are crazy old folks?" Cordelia edged up to help with the dish washing.

"Not at all." Sarah's hands stilled in the tepid water as she turned to give her mother-in-law a wide grin. "Why should Carrie and I have all the romance in the family?"

"I do love that old man excessively," Cordelia mused, looking years younger as her features soft-ened with the revelation. "Never thought I could love a man the way I loved the boys' father, but Eli took me unaware and here we are. I am only concerned about leaving you all."

"You needn't fear." Sarah grasped Cordelia's hand in the water. "We will surely settle nearby, and you will be worried to distraction by all the grandbabies. For now, we have a wedding to plan and a birthing to attend." Both women's gaze followed Carrie as she trundled by and they exchanged anticipatory grins. Sarah tampered the worry that would attend the latter event.

∞∞∞

Eli gave the command, "Let's roll!" The day's work began as the first wagon pushed over the ridge and, with brakes locked tight, began the controlled slide to the bottom. The men shouted and cajoled the oxen, against their will, to make the plunge. The women and children picked their way down on foot. It took the entire day to complete the descent, then the company rolled westward across the plain toward Dallas.

A day later Sarah took in the sights as they arrived in the crossroads of commerce for the buffalo and cattle trade. About 3,000 souls crowded along the Trinity River in this growing trade center on the Preston Trail heading north and south for delivery of cotton, hides and beef. What began as a trading post for both settlers and Indians; the town now welcomed thousands of refugees fleeing the destruction of the south.

"I never expected to see such crowds and commerce this far west."

"It is prospering along with the Fort, our last stop before we venture onto the plain. Just like we will prosper, Mrs. McKenna." Jacob shot her a wide grin.

"I have no doubt, my hardy pilgrim," Sarah laughed as she squeezed his muscled arm.

"Let's go find the love birds and see what the plans are to get them hitched." Jacob steered the wagon through the bustling crowd on the main street.

On the outskirts of town, they found the happy couple announcing their plans to the astonished and amused companions. The news was met with a bit of consternation on the part of several other older ladies who set their caps for the eligible widower.

"Well you sure set tongues to wagging with your bit of news," Jacob slapped Eli on the back.

"And I fear you have ruffled some hens' feathers as well," Sarah nodded toward the clutch of women whispering feverishly, heads locked together in a tight huddle.

"Don't mind them, we'll never see them again come Monday," Cordelia chuckled as she gave a little wave to the group, scattering them immediately.

"Did you locate a preacher?"

"We did, and he offered his church as well. We can have the ceremony after regular service Sunday afternoon."

"We've got a lot to do then, so let's get started." Sarah linked her arm in Cordelia's as they went to find Carrie to prepare for the joyful day.

SPACING

"You look like a schoolgirl ready for her first dance." Sarah adjusted the flowers in Cordelia's hair.

"I feel about as giddy." Cordelia surveyed her image in the full-length oval mirror in the church parlor.

"Did I ever tell you what your friendship and guidance have meant to me?" Sarah turned Cordelia to face her. "I don't know what I would have done had you not convinced me to follow Jacob. I could not see my way and you showed it to me, like Naomi to Ruth. I will be forever grateful."

"I will be forever grateful you took my advice, for you have made my somber son a new man." Cordelia gave her a tight squeeze.

"Time to go, can't keep the men waiting," Carrie appeared at the door.

Sarah and Carrie fell in behind Cordelia as she slowly made her way down the short aisle to a beaming Eli. The strains of Jacob's sweetly played wedding march filled the packed church. All the settlers were there to wish them well. Carrie and Sarah sang a romantic duet as the older couple stood with hands clasped and their eyes locked on one another. Jacob's warm, steady gaze caught Sarah's as the family grew to include Eli and James.

"I pronounce you man and wife," the parson announced, to the shouts of the gathered party and they spilled into the street toward camp, where a regular southern spread awaited.

Jacob slipped in behind the refreshment table and

tapped Sarah on the shoulder, almost upending the cup of punch she handed to a thirsty reveler.

"May I have this dance," he inquired, with a twinkle in his eye.

"So, the music taskmaster has given you a brief rest?" Sarah nodded toward Eli, who was making his way from the group of fiddlers to his bride.

"Said he couldn't wait one more note to get his hands on his beloved," Jacob laughed. "Told him I felt the same, so here I am."

Sarah nodded toward the dancers, "Looks like Gray has gotten into the spirit of the evening. He has tortured at least three of the girls."

Then she placed her hand in his and was whirled into the reel swinging by. Joy bubbled up from her into a responsive giggle.

Jacob romped her across the grass with abandon and she surrendered to his lead. As the reel slowed to a country waltz, he pulled her closer, into the full length of him.

"Mr. McKenna, we will scandalize the connections," she whispered up into his ear.

"Oh, I do hope so, Mrs. McKenna," he murmured, cinching her tighter. "Just announcing my claim."

His public display embarrassed and thrilled her, both at once.

As the slowing tempo of music rocked them, he loosened his grip into a soft caress. She lay her head over his heart as they swayed in perfect time.

"I love you, just in case you don't know," his

words rumbled through his chest into her heart. "I did not realize how much it would be so. When I was away where I could not protect you, I was worried how you would get along. I should have known you would meet the challenge, my brave frontier wife. I only hope you need me as much as I need you." He leaned in to peck her on her upturned nose.

"Don't be so quick with your praise. I failed at almost every task. I needed you so. If it had not been for the help of the others, I would have perished on the trail. I will gladly give you the lead in future where trailblazing is concerned, well, in other things as well." She gave up all pretense of holding the reigns of her family so tightly.

Eli maneuvered Cordelia across the crush of dancers to yell at Jacob. "Did you tell her our plan?"

"No, but guess I'll have to now," Jacob shot back.

"What plan is that?"

"Eli wants us all to take a cut of his land to stay close. What do you think?"

"What did you tell him?"

"I told him I would have to consult with my partner, my wife," Jacob grinned.

"Then partner, I say yes," Sarah laughed.

Jacob lifted her off the ground and swirled her around to seal the agreement.

"That seems an unreasonable price for a plain old

plow," Charles argued with the store manager, bargaining the price down as they shopped for provisions for their new homes.

"Skinning our hides, 'cause they know they can." Jacob came to stand beside Sarah as she longingly looked at the newest calico cloth being offered for an outrageous $4.00 per yard. She knew that in her new life she would probably never afford such a luxury again.

Jacob held up a particularly lovely golden piece. "Matches your hair."

She warmed in the light of his smile and knew also that she did not care that they could not afford such frills. She had Jacob and her family and, as Cordelia said many months ago, that was all that mattered.

They loaded new supplies to last at least six months, along with new farm implements bought with the last of their stash of cash. They were truly on the land now and eager to get started in order to get in a growing season before fall.

The full company gathered one last time to say their first farewells to those leaving the train early. It was a tearful affair.

"Now folks, gather 'round as we bless those leaving our company." Eli gathered the flock in around the first wagon.

"Lord Almighty, bless those that go out from our camp today. Give them health and prosperity. Guard their character so we can meet again on the other side. We ask it in the name of your blessed son

Jesus. Amen."

The crowd dispersed to their wagons and Eli and Jacob mounted up and the command to roll the train was given for the last time. Folks waved until their friends were no longer in sight as the wagons split off into three directions.

Chapter 21

Those westward bound spent the morning being ferried across the Trinity, swollen from spring rains. Then it was on to Fort Worth. The fort was no longer a military outpost but a cattle town, like Dallas. Out beyond was the frontier, Indian land.

"You sure the Indians are peaceable?" Sarah worried.

"Most have been removed further west and north, so I hear they are not seen much these days," Jacob reassured her.

"I heard some talk of recent raids while we were in Dallas."

"I did as well but we are here, and we will have to rely on God for our safety. He has brought us this far. He will not abandon us," Jacob reminded her of God's care through the recent months. She had been sure God had abandoned her, and her family, but now here she sat with at least five new members to her household plus others to come. God had surely blessed, bringing good from deep sorrow. She smiled at the thought of His management of her life when she could not see her way clearly.

Later in the afternoon, just outside the fort perimeter, Charles hallooed from his wagon for Jacob to pull out and stop.

He called out as he ran forward, "It's Carrie. I think it's her time." He was out of breath from the sprint and excitement.

Sarah barreled off the box to go to her sister. "Cordelia, your medicine bag. Carrie is laboring."

As she reached the wagon behind, she could hear her sister moaning softly in the back. She stepped up and inside to find Carrie rolling from side to side, clutching her belly. "How long Carrie, how long have you been in pain?"

"Since morning. It was not so bad then and I did not want to hold up the train but," she stopped to gasp, then moaned as the pain engulfed her. "But now, I am afraid. It hurts more than I imagined." She grasped for Sarah's hand. "Help me."

"Oh, my dear, it will be alright. We're here." Sarah choked back the fear threatening and began preparations to deliver the first McKenna of a new generation in the Texas mesquite brush. This was how it was going to be from now on, fighting the land and elements to carve out a new life. A spirit of determination gripped her. She could do this.

Cordelia clambered into the tight space and with efficiency examined Carrie, eliciting a stronger cry of pain. "We don't have time to get to the fort, this is the place my grandchild has chosen to make an entrance." She set to work mixing a mild sedative that soon had Carrie more at ease but only for a time, then the heavy labor commenced.

∞ ∞ ∞

The men paced outside, busying themselves making a hasty camp. The fort was in sight, so they felt it safe to stop in order to let nature take its course.

"I can't stand to hear her in such pain. I swear I will never touch her again," Charles declared as he plopped into the dust dropping his head into his hands.

"Now brother, don't be too hasty there. Once she is done, she will quickly forget the pain and only set her heart on the babe and then, soon enough again, you," Eli chuckled, keeping the conversation light-hearted and upbeat.

The cries coming from the wagon were un-nerving to Jacob as well. Women must be the bravest creatures on this Earth. He gave a quick thought to keeping his hands off his bride if this was going to be the result, but he knew he could never do it.

Runwell began a frantic bark focused behind Charles.

"Rattler, don't move!" Gray charged up behind Charles and pinned the serpent to the ground with a hoe blade. The men stood and scouted the area dis-patching several more of the deadly snakes.

"Another one over here!" Jacob jumped out of striking distance as Gray swung the fatal blow.

"We are on the prairie now, a man needs to watch his step," Charles quipped nervously.

The men continued to reconnoiter, guarding the perimeter of the camp.

Evening wore into night and still the struggle in and out of the wagon continued. Sarah emerged to fetch another pan of water that the men had boiled.

"Why so long? Is all well?" Jacob asked as she headed back.

"All is well, it is her first, it just takes longer." Sarah could sense the fear in his demeanor and hoped to ease it.

Jacob held her gaze, communicating without words his love and support. She felt strengthened by the exchange and plunged back into the ordeal.

As sunrise painted the sky with unique Texas brilliance, the first cries of the newborn McKenna replaced those of the mother. Charles scrambled into the wagon as Cordelia and Sarah rolled out in happy exhaustion.

∞∞∞∞

Jacob caught Sarah as she stood up and kissed her hard. All his fear, frustration and admiration were packed into the exchange. When he let her up for air, his fierce gaze held her still.

"Kill any snakes while I was gone, my brave frontiersman?" Sarah teased to break the tension.

"Birth any babes, my dear frontierswoman?" Jacob answered.

Charles emerged from the wagon with his son

and showed him off to all.

"What name have you saddled him with?" Gray gently fingered the swaddling blanket to get a better look at his new nephew.

"Well, my sweet wife and I have taken a liking to our last stop, Dallas. Seeing as how our boy seemed to want to see it before we moved on, we thought we'd just name him after his birthplace." Charles lifted his son to the dawn sky. "Dallas, meet the world." Laughter and good wishes rang out over the prairie.

After a hearty breakfast, Sarah and Jacob strolled arm in arm up the road stopping to catch a glimpse of Fort Worth in the distance. Jacob gathered his love into his arms and kissed her long and deliberately. He sobered, thinking where his kiss might naturally lead. He pulled back and searched Sarah's sweet face and voiced his thought, "Aren't you afraid of where this might lead?"

"What, of a natural function?" Sarah teased the frown on his lips.

"The pain, the risk," Jacob continued as he worried her lips with his own.

"God made woman for such work." Sarah pressed closer.

"Sarah, I am serious." Jacob broke the embrace. "I could not stand to lose you, not even for my own child."

"Well, my brave frontiersman, that is just a chance you will have to take." Sarah beamed at him and then laughed full out as she smoothed her palms over her skirt front.

It took a moment for the slight gesture to sink in, then for the shock to pass. He swung her into his arms and danced down the road. All fear was forgotten, replaced with joy of the knowledge that he was going to be a father.

∞∞∞

The McKennas rolled into Fort Worth amid travelers from North, South, and East. The streets teemed with immigrants, cattlemen, soldiers, and the first sight of plains Indians they had heard tales of. Jacob guided his team, following the stream of wagons out to the west of town, soon locating the remainder of their group camped along-side a small creek. The bright supper fires greeted their arrival and, once the word spread that there was a new name on the train roster, all the travelers gathered to get a look at the new member of the party.

"We hear you got some news to tell." Eli slapped Jacob on the shoulder, almost dislodging him from the convenient stump he had come to rest on. The men urged Jacob to spill it.

"Well, if you must know, my beautiful bride over there," he gestured to a beaming Sarah being surrounded and congratulated by the women a distance away, "she tells me that I am going to be a father come fall."

The men erupted in laughter and teasing hoots at the good news.

"So, with Cordelia being a Grandma, you gonna be a Grandpa Eli?" Stovall nudged Eli for an answer.

"Yeah, I suppose so. Jacob and Sarah have agreed to take a section of our land, like Charles and Carrie, so we can keep the clan together."

As the women offered their best child-rearing advice to the new mothers, the men exchanged directions to their properties to the west and their plans for a future of plentiful crops and livestock, the dream of all the displaced families flooding into this vast new land.

The group gathered the next morning to have breakfast together. As they finished the meal Eli stood to give them their last charge to go forth and prosper. Then he led them in singing the old parting hymn, *"Blessed be the tie that binds."*

Sarah knew it would be a long time before she would lift her voice in a choral group again and she took advantage to savor the harmonies as the singers broke into the memorized parts. There was not a dry eye or heart unmoved. She would never forget those who struggled to reach this new land with them. Nor would she forget those lain by along the way or back on scarred battlefields throughout the south.

Once more the settlers waved and hallooed their goodbyes as the wagons moved off in all directions. Sarah felt a shiver of trepidation as their three lone teams pushed westward out onto the prairie. The vastness of the land came into focus for her as she scanned the horizon in all directions and saw not one sign of civilized habitation. Their wagons seemed to be three small boats on a huge green ocean, alone and vulnerable. A day's travel brought them to a rise in the land. As they topped it, a fertile valley stretched before them as far as the eye could see. A river snaked through gently waving grass, offering blessed fresh water in opposition to the previously arid landscape. Runwell darted down the rise leaping into the green carpet.

"Well, how do you like your new home?" Eli rode up pointing ahead. "See that little copse of trees to the north. That is my sister's place. And the sections to the south are ours." He panned his hand to the green grassland sliced by the tree-lined river flowing southward.

Sarah knew what the Children of Israel must have felt as they surveyed the land of Canaan. It was more beautiful than she had imagined; beautiful and intimidating and dangerous but theirs for the taking.

Jacob pulled her close and placed a kiss on the top of her head. "Our new home, Mrs. McKenna."

Jacob came to stand behind Sarah as she knelt on the ground digging a hole that she carefully surveyed for correct distance from the half constructed soddy and the river. She eyed and walked the spot for days. She nursed a dogwood cutting that reminded her of Jacob's tender loving in the east Texas woods, the joining that created the sweet life growing inside her. In days ahead when the hard times threatened to beat down her memories of their first love, she would look out the tiny window and see the dogwood, symbol of life, and remember.

"What on earth are you planting now?" He mused over her head.

"This cutting from the dogwood tree," Sarah carefully unwrapped the small twig and laid it beside another small bundle.

"And which tree would that be?" Jacob teased. He knew full well which tree as he had fond memories of it too.

He watched her work as he continued to muse on all she had done since coming into this untamed land. She carefully laid out the placement of her peach seeds and planted her orchard. She trimmed and squared the mud bricks he cut from the riverbank to build their one-room sod home. She hauled water, expertly cooked whatever game he offered over the open fire, kept their quickly fraying clothes washed and mended. Jacob appreciated her southern farm girl skills that were an asset to the establishment of their homestead. The framework of a working farm was being erected as they toiled without complaint to build their dream. He especially appreciated that she came to him freely in the night, when the wild sounds of the land could turn back the hardiest of adventurers. She accepted his love and comfort until the dawn of a new day. He thanked God for he was truly blessed.

She smiled up at him and put his thoughts to words. "God has truly blessed us. Though I do not understand why we had to suffer so, He has worked it for good, as He promised." She bent back to her work.

Jacob watched, amused, as she unwrapped the second bundle to reveal the clod of Mississippi mud she nursed over three states and a thousand miles. She allowed Runwell a sniff then she carefully placed it into the hole. She stood the twig on top and began to cover the hole with moist native dirt. "I claim this land as our home with the transfer of Mississippi mud to Texas prairie dirt." Sarah concluded her playful ceremony with a flourish of final sprinkles. She stood and turned to her beloved. "You think it will take?"

He looked into her shining eyes and placed his hand over her small mounding belly. He thought of the new generation to come as he pronounced, "Everything we plant in this new land is going to take, Mrs. McKenna." Then he swung her into his arms and, with Runwell nipping at their heels, he waltzed her around the tiny twig that promised to blossom in their new home in the Big Valley of Texas.

I hope you enjoyed Sarah and Jacob's story. It was born from, and loosely based on, my interest and research into a true account from my family history. These are some of the things I thought about as I learned of these first pioneers of Parker County, Texas.

Questions to consider after reading *Sarah's Chance*:

☐☐ Are you more likely to view personal hardship as a punishment or a refining fire? What does God's Word say about it?

☐☐ If you had to leave your generational home and pack only the most precious items that you could carry in a small container, what would you choose?

☐☐ What about your home would you most hate to leave?

☐☐ If you had to decide to marry a man you had only known a short while, what character traits would you consider in favor of the decision? Against?

☐☐ Considering the current refugee populations displaced by war, compare/contrast the world today with that of the post-Civil-War era. What are some of the similarities in the difficulties that they face?

Books In This Series

Willows by the Watercourses

Willows by the Watercourses is a three book series following three generations of related women...Sarah, Kit and Lily as they move onto the Texas frontier, find love and fill the land with their families—like "willows by the watercourses".

3 For I will pour water on him who is thirsty, and floods upon dry ground. I will pour my Spirit upon thy seed, and my blessing upon thine offspring:
4 And they shall spring up as among the grass, as willows by the watercourses. Isaiah 44: 3-4

Sarah's Chance - 1

Sarah Partin cries out to God for direction as she reads the letter telling that a fifth brother has died in service to the Confederacy. The men of the family are gone. She is numb from repeated blows of grief and exhausted from the struggle to keep the farm going with just her younger sister and brother to help.

Jacob McKenna, a refugee Confederate soldier passing through town headed to Texas, answers Sarah's advertisement for field hands to plant and harvest. He must hire himself out to get better shelter for his mother and wounded brother and to build a cash stake for the journey to a new life in a new land.

Kit's Challenge - 2 *** See Excerpt In The Following Pages***

Challenges of Indian relations, tensions between ranchers and farmers, and the harsh life on the Texas frontier are threatening widow Kit Cooper's struggles to raise four young sons and to hold onto her land. Her relationship with former Indian captive Joshua Reynolds raises questions in the minds of the townfolk and in her heart. When she discovers he harbours a secret concerning the torture and death of her father, can she find the grace to forgive?

Lily's Call - 3

Lily Reynolds arrives on the last American frontier, the Texas High Plains, for her first teaching assignment. She must navigate relations between the farmers and ranchers while wrangling their children to the disciplines of reading, writing and arithmetic.

Tensions are equally strained between the Anglos and Mexican laborers needed to work the fields and livestock.

When Gabriel Aragon, an XIT foreman, requests that the children of his Mexican hands be allowed to attend school, a struggle between the two cultures erupts, with Lily in the middle.

Her mission is to educate children, not to regulate disputes between adults. She must discover why God called her to this hard task in such a desolate place.

About The Author

Lauren Jan Craft

Hello Readers...
I hope you enjoyed journeying with Sarah and Jacob and their families onto the wide open prairie of Texas. Their story is based on true tales of loves in my family that lasted a lifetime. The letters in the story are real, penned by the brother of Sarah, Carrie and Gray before he died, in his fourth year of service in the Confederate army, at the Battle of Atlanta. He was indeed the last of five brothers to die, leaving the sisters and younger brother to embark on the difficult journey to Texas. Their story so moved me that I had to tell it. Of couse much of my version was fictionalized by inference from research into the main threads I discovered. I feel the ending was happy as the families were successful in Texas where most descendants still live.

Today we are living in a difficult time. However, I believe just as William wrote in one of twenty-five letters to Sarah, with dates spaning from 1861 to just before his death in 1864, "the darkest night is just before dawn". Our hardship is no more than our ancestors endured.

While we wait for the light, I hope you will continue to follow the Texas trail in the next two books, mostly fiction sprinkled with bits of historical facts about life on the plains in the late 19th century. Enjoy a sneak peek at the next generation of related family in Kit's Challenge coming in the Winter, 2021. If you liked Sarah and Jacob's story, please consider leaving a review at Amazon, Good Reads or related sites.

I would love to hear from you so please feel free to contact me at:

Website: laurenjancraft.net

Facebook :Lauren Jan Craft

Email: laurenjancraft@gmail.com

Blessings to you and yours!
Lauren Jan Craft

Kit's Challenge

Kitty Cooper pulled herself to standing in the muck and squinted up to the sunlit hole she'd punched in the poorly covered opening above the pit. Tears of frustration stung the backs of her eyes. Early that morning she wrestled her four young sons out of bed and fed them their meager breakfast of oat cakes. Then they grudgingly piled onto Buster the mule who would deliver them safely down the road to school. She padded out in her chemise to check again to see if the ornery hen offered up any eggs. None were there at six when she needed them. As she scuffed across the dirt and gravel yard toward the chicken house, lost in dark thoughts, she made a mental note that things could not get any worse.

Things got worse.

Now she stood down the half-dug well in her nightdress, knee deep in mud and not a soul for miles to hear her until her sons return later in the afternoon.

Then she remembered. Josh Reynolds is coming this morning for the peaches.

"Lord, have mercy," she groaned.

"Mrs. Cooper?" Right on time, Kitty heard Mr. Reynolds calling. She could answer and be saved from the muck now or wait until the boys got home in about seven hours. She shivered from the shock of the fall, wet from the waist down. The thought of Josh Reynolds seeing her in such a state of undress, and covered in mud, was mortifying. But she had learned over the two years since her husband's death that beggars can't be choosers and to be grateful for God's providence. At the moment Josh Reynolds was provided as her rescuer and sometimes she needed one to pull her back from the brink of despair.

"Over here," she yelled to the sky above.

"Mrs. Cooper?" Josh moved toward the phantom voice.

"I'm about fifty paces from the house to the chicken yard, down a hole," Kit yelled back. She could hear a vague shuffle on the rocky dirt above. Then Mr. Reynolds peered down at her.

Saved.

"There's rope in the barn hanging by the door," she shouted.

He didn't answer, just followed her direction to procure the rope.

Within moments the rope snaked down toward Kit and she shimmied up like her brothers taught her when she tagged behind them as they roamed the arroyos and draws. Josh offered her a hand up as she broke the rim of the pit. He kept his eyes averted.

"Thank-you, Mr. Reynolds. If you will wait just a moment I will get the preserves," Kit stated in as dignified a speech as she could muster in the circumstance. Then she stiffly marched to the house and disappeared inside.

Josh Reynolds rarely smiled but his lips twitched in effort to suppress the rare gesture of amusement as his gaze followed her ram-rod march to her back door. He took care with his thoughts but he couldn't help but note that she was everything that pleased him. She was medium height, curves in all the right places, long hair like corn-silk and eyes the color of a spring sky. He had long admired Kit Cooper. Her dignified address as she stood covered with mud underlined the frontier grit of the woman. He interacted with her often as she brought in peaches, preserves, and hand-stitched items to sell at his store. The relationship was formal, as it was with all of the town's folk.

"Mrs. Cooper, I gotta go up the road a piece to the Barton's. I can come back on my way into town," Josh called at the back door, thinking she might need a little time to compose herself before doing business.

"That would be fine, Mr. Reynolds. I'll see you later," Kit yelled back.

When he returned around three o'clock, Kit greeted him in her usual composed manner. Her hair was scraped back into a tight braid coiled at the back of her head. The severity of the style emphasized her large blue eyes in a too thin face. Just as they concluded business, a ruckus outside interrupted.

"Ma," Ben called. "Ma, John's hurt!"

Josh and Kit hurried out the door to find three brothers helping the fourth down from Buster. Blood covered the boy's face and stained the front of his shirt.

"Oh, John, were you fighting again?" Kit asked as she examined his forehead.

Three boys piped up at once to defend him.

"Wasn't his fault, Ma," Ben began.

"Thierry Barton followed behind us coming home," Will added.

"He said his Pa would have our land," Sam stated. "John just said when hell froze over."

"Sam, watch your mouth. Did you say that, John?" Kit queried, inspecting the thin, bloody split above John's right eye.

"Yes ma'am, I did. Then he came off his horse and so did I," John admitted.

"And," Kit coaxed.

"John gave him a kick in the shin," Sam grunted, kicking up a cloud of dust with the toe of his boot.

"Then Thierry tripped John and jumped on him and wouldn't let him up," Will said soberly as he put a calming hand on Sam's shoulder.

"I had to pull him off and we blocked him from jumping John again until he decided he didn't want to fight the three of us." Ben continued the story as he stepped forward to help John up the steps.

Josh followed the clutch of Coopers into the house, the boys crowded around their mother like chicks around a biddy hen. He heard her soft-spoken, sensible admonitions delivered as she moved about the neat-as-a-pin main room, gathering supplies to minister to her bloodied son.

"Boys, you know it is best to use words not fists," Kit said as she dabbed at the bright red trickle sliding down John's cheek. "The Bible tells us to resist striking at our enemies."

"Begging your pardon, ma'am, but there comes a time when a man must stand against a bully or the provocations will never stop." Josh was as shocked as the fair Mrs. Cooper by his sudden interjection into the conversation. He had not meant to speak his thoughts aloud.

She froze in mid-stride to stare at him. "And how do you propose one might stop a bully?"

"Always be prepared to defend yourself and if the time comes, use your skills to make your intention clear," Josh explained.

"And what skills would those be?" Kit answered, propping her hands on her hips.

"Well it seems that John here was on the receiving end of Thierry's skills so it might behoove him to learn to give as well as take," Josh countered, rising to the challenge.

"You mean fisticuffs," Kit returned, cocking an eyebrow.

"Well, not precisely," Josh drew out his words with a hint of mystery.

"And where will he learn these skills?" she inquired, with a slight quirk to the hard line of her mouth.

"Well, I could show him, and his brothers, a few tricks I know," Josh offered, hoping she would agree.

Kit seemed to roll the idea around in her thoughts

before she spoke, "A case of peaches for lessons for my boys, Mr. Reynolds." She looked him in the eye as she presented her offer to barter for his services as an instructor in the art of taming bullies.

Recognizing her pride in play he accepted, even though he would have done it for free. "Deal," he sealed the bargain.

The boys stilled as they observed the exchange between the imposing man and their mother. When the deal was concluded, they broke stance with whoops of anticipation of the tricks they might learn.

Josh stood back and watched as Kit ministered to her wounded warrior. His mind wandered to Sky Bird and her tender ministrations that he received after raids with his Comanche brothers. Kit finished her task and he blinked as he watched her lean forward placing a soft kiss on her son's forehead just as Sky Bird had done. Unexpected longing shot through him leaving him a bit off balance.

"Mr. Reynolds, when should we expect you to begin your proposed lessons," Kit asked, coming into clear focus.

He didn't want to leave but if courtesy, and the jumbled state of his thoughts, dictated he should, he wanted to return as soon as possible. "Tomorrow, after school?" he answered.

"Yes, yes, Mama, can he?" The boys bounced around her begging an affirmative answer.

Kit laughed. "Yes, I suppose we need to get to work on your skills as soon as possible," she agreed, smiling up at Josh.

His breath caught in the light of her smile. "Tomorrow then, at four," he answered and turned to go.

"Mr. Reynolds, you forgot the peaches," she reminded him of his original mission.

He stepped over to the table and picked up the crate holding the golden preserves, staring over her head, not daring to look back into her eyes.

Kit watched him go with some confusion. He seemed tense as he left.

Kit observed from her perch on the porch as Josh demonstrated the choreographed wrestling moves to her awe struck sons. The large man became stealthy as a mountain lion as he crouched to move in on his prey. Kit recognized the style as that of the plains Indians that still populated the area, although most were in reserves to the North now. The moves would serve her sons well as they would surprise most of their tormenters. The bullies would not learn Indian fighting due to their prejudices. Kit had no such aversions. Born and raised in Comancheria, she knew good and bad people came in all stripes. Atrocities were not the signature of only one group. In short, life on the plains was complicated. Her parents taught her to measure people based on their personal actions and character. She was teaching her sons to do the same. Many shunned Josh Reynolds due to his upbringing by the most savage of the plains tribes, the Kiowa Apache then later the Comanche. His Indian captive background, at once, made him an acknowledged Texas frontiersman and a curiosity. He straddled both worlds and belonged to neither. By all accounts, his integration back into his family was difficult. He was completely assimilated into the groups that captured him. She did not know all the details, just noticed the surreptitious whispers behind cupped hands when Josh appeared in church or on the street. He did not attend the social affairs of the community. But she always found him calm and fair in his dealings with her. She watched him now as he gently and patiently led her boys through the unfamiliar wrestling stances. She felt confident in her decision to let Joshua Reynolds take on the tutoring of her sons.

"You boys practice what I showed you and I will be back next week to show you more," Josh gave instructions over the pleas of the boys to continue as he dusted off his hands and clothes.

"Boys, tell Mr. Reynolds thank-you and go get washed up," Kit ordered. Her brood obeyed immediately.

"Your boys learn quickly. They will be good fighters when I am done," Josh observed.

"Well, I hope they temper it with good judgment. There is a time to fight but also a time to reason," Kit countered.

"I will give them the skills to fight when necessary and hopefully you will give them the character to know when temperance is the best move. You seem to have a good start on that. They are good boys," Josh said as he stopped just feet from her.

His compliment flowed onto her like warm sunlight on a cold stone. It had been a long time since she had any positive indication concerning her parenting of four rambunctious boys. She more often got glares as her son's exuberance got the better of them and the tranquil peace of some town folk was interrupted. She had no idea whether she was doing a good job or not and a fair amount of her mental energy was spent worrying about whether she was raising saints or hellions.

"Thank you, Mr. Reynolds. I hope you are right," she said as she bowed her head.

"You can be certain of it," Josh reassured. She seemed to need the affirmation and he only stated his observations. She had a good handle on her boys. They immediately followed her command; no back-talk, no sass. They were adventuresome but that's just boys. And in a quartet, the mayhem was magnified. He did not see any meanness or mischief in their activities, just true frontier kids, tough and independent.

"Same time next week," Josh asked.

"That will be fine," Kit answered.

He grabbed his hat from the porch, tipped it after he adjusted it on his head and reluctantly moved to his horse. Kit Cooper seemed so vulnerable out here on the plain, ten miles from town. He knew most of the land was safe now but he was aware that some raiding parties still resisted going into the reservations. There had not been any trouble in a long time but as long as the renegade bands remained the potential was there. Then there was the threat from her neighbors, the Bartons. As cattle ranchers they were incorporating, by any means, all the free land and many of the hard scrabble small homesteads in the area. Kit had been threatened repeatedly but she tenaciously held onto her acreage in the face of terrible odds. Inexplicably, he felt responsible for her but knew she would not appreciate or accept his interference. He would have to continue to disguise his help as he didn't seem to be able to leave her to fate and no one else seemed to be stepping up to help.

He rode back into town from the opposite direction to Kit's farm as he knew his visits could compromise her reputation in this closed community. Josh remembered the first time he really observed Kit Cooper. She stood shivering with her boys in a cold spring rain as the town came out to bury her young husband. She was stoic as they sang and the preacher read the words committing her husband to the ground. Many town folks offered help then but over time as the town grew, filling with strangers from the four corners of the country, she was more and more left on her own. He gave brief thought to approaching her openly with a personal offer of help but his courage failed him. She would never accept such help and out of respect he honored her fierce fight for independence. He began to quietly look after her and her boys in his own way by providing her goods and services in his store at a carefully disguised discount. He dealt with her weekly as she brought in produce, hand-stitched items, and her delicious peach preserves in order to make ends meet. Their exchanges were perfunctory, related to the business at hand. His admiration for her grew but he did not know how to approach her. In the Indian way, his first wife was given to him as a gift for service rendered. He knew nothing about courtship. He was lucky that Sky Bird had been a perfect mate for him in his other life. They shared a great love and he was bereft when she and his son died. But he had no idea how to approach a woman in this world.

"Here you are." Mrs. Matilda Barton exclaimed as she entered the store. "I came by yesterday and you were closed by four." She fixed her gimlet glare on him.

"I had some business to attend to." Josh answered patiently.

"Seems inconsiderate to neglect your customers," Mrs. Barton muttered under her breath.

"Well, what can I do to make amends?" Josh placated. He helped her with her purchases as the store filled with speculating customers. He never shut his doors early. He made a mental note to go out to the Cooper's later in future.

"Mornin', Josh," Colton Reed said as he sauntered to the counter. "Need some shells."

Josh answered as he reached for the ammunition, "Going huntin' Colt?"

"Yeah, for some renegades up Jacksboro way, they stole some horses and burned a barn. No life lost but they are gettin' bolder and need to be checked," Colt said as he began stuffing the ammo into his bag.

"Kiowa or Comanch?" Josh asked.

"Comanch, don't think you know this bunch. They are some young toughs thinking they can break out of the reservation and reclaim the land. No offense Josh, but those days are gone," Colt answered as he paid for his purchase.

"None taken Colt; coming from you," Josh stated. He liked the sheriff and knew that while he did his duty, Colt acknowledged the complicated nature of the relations between the conquered Indians and the settlers flooding over their land.

"Oh, and by the way, better ride a little further out and around when comin' home from Kit Cooper's place. People might talk," Colt teased dryly with a twinkle in his eye.

"Much obliged for your advice," Josh answered, aggravated to be caught.

Kit entered the store as Colt left and walked determinedly to the counter. Josh noted the lull in the conversation of the other customers as he watched her, and her boys, cross the distance from the door.

"I have brought some handkerchiefs to sell," she offered.

"Good. I am about out of your last set. Same price as before?" he answered.

"That will be fine, Mr. Reynolds," she accepted.

The boys mingled close by, eyeing the penny candy under the counter.

"We been practicing, Mr. Reynolds," Sam announced.

Josh looked in the direction of the ladies at the fabric table. He knew they were listening. "That's good,

Sam," he answered.

"John got Ben in a choke hold and wouldn't let him up," Sam continued as he stepped out from his Mama's skirts.

"Did not," Ben argued, defending himself.

"Did so," Sam exclaimed as he took a firmer stance, his fists balled.

"I let him up when he squealed," John said as he picked up a piece of candy and inspected it.

"Boys, stop," Kit intervened.

"Yes Ma'am," the boys chimed and circled in closer.

Josh looked steadily at the women behind Kit as he offered, "Boys would you like to pick a piece of candy, one each."

"Oh, yes, thank-you Mr. Reynolds," they replied politely, in chorus.

"I will pay, Mr. Reynolds," Kit insisted as she began digging into her small bag. She seemed to detect the glare of the ladies at her back.

"No, the treat is on me. The boys earned it with their practice," he said, smiling. The cackle birds twittered excitedly as if they had discovered a fat juicy worm to devour.

Josh knew he would be sorry he ignited the speculation between the town gossips but he did not care at that moment as he watched the boys carefully choose their very rare treat. He burned in the warmth of the delighted smile of their mother.

Chapter 2

Kit stopped her assault on the washboard to watch as her boys practiced the moves Joshua Reynolds taught them, stirring up a cloud of dust as they rough-housed over the rocky dirt. She looked past her scuffling brood to the fields beyond. The boys were older, stronger now, but it would still be a struggle to bring in the wheat harvest in June and the cotton in September.

She mentally conversed with God in her casual way, "Lord, please send some help. I am not sure I can do this again this year." Just as she finished the thought, Mr. Reynolds broke the rise coming toward the house. He had an uncanny way of turning up lately when her thoughts turned to possible defeat in her efforts to carry on in her fight to keep the farm and family going.

The boys scattered and ran toward the man with obvious delight. She had a surprising urge to do the same. He came each week to instruct her boys just as he had promised. She began to look forward to his visits. She rationalized that the sessions broke the usual drudge of hard life on the plains.

Mrs. Cooper," Joshua said as he slid out of the saddle and tipped his hat to her. The boys clamored around him.

"Mr. Reynolds," she answered, squinting in the bright sunlight, her hand over her brow.

"Ready boys?" he acknowledged the crowd around him. "Have you been practicing?"

"Yes sir." The clot of boys and man moved away from her.

Kit felt a bit of envy as Josh's attention became entirely focused on the boys and the lesson began. She peeked between the damp sheets and fresh-washed clothes as the yelping and cajoling ensued. While Mr. Reynolds patiently coaxed her boys to controlled ferocity she took a break from the back-breaking scrubbing to just sit and watch. He spoke with authority, but gently, as he gave instructions and the boys listened with rapt attention then carried out the orders with earnest effort. Each of the boys took a turn at the adversary.

She could not help but observe the man's physical form and strength. He was tall and broadly built but moved with cat-like grace. His blond shoulder-length hair framed a darkly tanned face. His grass-green eyes were sharp and aware. Although not classically handsome he was striking in appearance. Kit enjoyed watching the dance he did with her boys but felt a slight unease in acknowledging it. She just knew that she wanted the visits to continue.

After an hour of hard scrabble wrestling the group retreated to the shade of the porch to rest. Kit drew a pail of water and offered them all a drink.

"Your boys are good wrestlers, Mrs. Cooper," Josh observed.

"Please call me Kit, Mr. Reynolds. I consider you a close enough friend with all the help you have given to me and mine," Kit instructed.

"If you will call me Josh," Josh answered, his gaze was intense. Kit had to look away in self-defense.

"Josh," Kit stopped to adjust to the intimacy of using his informal name. She did not want him to leave. She needed some adult conversation, she reasoned. "Would you like to stay to supper?"

It was his turn to be surprised. He did not expect her to invite him into her home in any other capacity but business. No one else would. He was not sure he should accept as it might compromise her if the town folks noticed their more familiar relationship. And he did not trust himself to keep the growing awareness of her as more than a friend from becoming apparent. But a home cooked meal was hard to turn down.

"That would be real nice, Mrs.—Kit," he replied giving in to the strong urge to stay. "C'mon boys, we've got about an hour more light. I got another trick or two to show you."

"Mr. Reynolds, when you gonna show how to knife throw?" John asked.

"Well, I've got my knife right here. We will have to ask your mother," Josh directed the question to Kit.

"I never thought of knife throwing as an essential skill. I am afraid they might get hurt," she redirected, her big blues eyes searching his for an explanation.

"Well, it is not technically, but it could come in handy if you want to hit something at a distance, maybe a snake?" he teased. He loved the way she kept a straight face but the glint in her eye met his challenge.

"Well, in that case you may proceed," she gave in with a smile as the boys gave a whoop.

Josh pulled out his battle worn weapon and started with the safety rules first. Then he moved on to tricks for aiming and good throwing technique. As he demonstrated he became more uneasy as memories of the times he actually used his knife flooded into his mind and snakes had not been the target. He knew he should not be entertaining ideas about Kit Cooper because if she knew his violent past she would be as repulsed as the rest of the town folks. As he concluded his demonstration he decided not to let the boys handle the knife just yet. He needed to rethink how to teach such a skill that would stress peaceful purposes.

"Aw, please, Mr. Reynolds, just one throw," the boys begged.

"Not today boys, maybe next time," Josh answered as he sheathed the evocative weapon.

"Go wash up," Kit interrupted just in time.

Josh followed the boys to the pump and splashed cool water on his face and neck and tidied up as best he could, then followed the boys into the house.

The table was set with a cloth, a fistful of fragrant spring flowers graced a preserve jar in the center. He wondered if these niceties were a rule in the Cooper house. Kit indicated a place at the head of the table, a surprise, and they all sat down. The boys immediately clasped hands and Kit gestured that he might join the circle. He offered his hand and she gently took it and bowed her head.

"Heavenly Father, we thank you for this blessed day. We ask you to bless the food to the nourishment of our bodies. We ask you to bless Mr. Reynolds as he has come to help us in our need. In sweet Jesus' name, Amen," Kit finished, releasing his hand immediately and he keenly felt the loss. He was humbled by the blessing of this woman who had nothing herself but prayed to God to bless him. She quietly circled the table ladling red beans with tiny bits of bacon into their bowls. Then she brought a pan of golden corn-bread to the table and sat down.

"Ma, special beans," Sam piped up excitedly.

"Yes, Sam, now eat," Kit ordered.

Josh noted the meager fare. A flood of protective anger washed over him. He wanted to pick his bowl clean of those precious bits and give these boys every bite. He wanted to protect their mother from the harsh life in which she was trapped. The love they shared was not going to be enough in the long haul. They needed a man to help with the endless chores, a man to protect them from dangers inherent in life on the frontier, a man to fight for them when necessary.

Semi-finalist 2016 - ACFW Genesis Contest